FAITHF...

By

ANNA MARKLAND

COVER ART BY STEVEN NOVAK

COPYRIGHT

"Sail away from the safe harbor.
Catch the trade winds in your sails.
Explore. Dream. Discover."
~Mark Twain

For the men, women and children
who cannot find peace though the war may be over.

SKIMMING STONES

Island of Chersos, Dalmatia, 1139 AD

Konrad von Wolfenberg wouldn't have revealed anything of his difficult past to his swarthy interrogator if he'd foreseen Drosik's sarcastic disbelief. When would he learn to keep his mouth shut?

The diminutive captain whose crew he sought to join made no effort to conceal his amusement. "You were destined to be a priest, and now you want to be a pirate," he crowed for the fifth time.

Kon supposed he couldn't blame Drosik. He didn't fully understand himself how his path in life had changed drastically.

Hoping to provide a distraction, he braced his booted feet in the sand, bent his knees, leaned back and skimmed a pebble across the waters of the Adriatic—still and calm for once. "It's a long story."

Drosik jumped down from his perch atop a boulder and picked up a rock. He closed one eye and stuck out his tongue, then tried and failed to match the six splashes. Kon wasn't surprised. It was obvious from the way the Dalmatian had chosen the pebble at random he hadn't been perfecting the skill since the age of four.

The memory transported Kon back to happier times—their patient father teaching him and Lute and Johann, and even Sophia, how to choose the best stones to skim across the waters of the Elbe. To the annoyance of her brothers, Sophia had proven to be the most adept.

It seemed long ago and far away, a lifetime. Each of his siblings was happily married and well settled. Johann might by now have inherited the prestigious title of Count von Wolfenberg. Their heartbroken father wasn't expected to survive his beloved wife by long.

Kon had been driven to leave the home he loved shortly after his mother's death, though he had to admit he wasn't certain what the driving force was. Perhaps he'd believed that if he left Saxony he'd rediscover the ability to feel grief, or any emotion. Or mayhap the real Konrad still lay buried beneath the deadly rockfall in the Pale Mountains during the imperial army's long retreat from Italy.

"We Narentines have been celebrated pirates for centuries," Drosik declared, brushing off the rumpled sleeves of the brightest red shirt

Kon had ever seen, apparently undismayed at his lack of skimming prowess.

"Really," Kon replied, his thoughts still in Saxony. "I assumed a man who lived on the sea would be an expert skimmer."

Drosik shrugged, apparently taking no offence at the jest. "I was too busy learning to be a sailor." He thrust out his chest. "I am named for Drosaico, a great Narentine pirate captain who signed a peace treaty with the cursed Venetians more than a hundred years ago."

Kon scoffed. "Peace treaty! Evidently it didn't last."

His companion scowled. "What kind of world would it be if Dalmatians didn't raid Venetian ships? Venezia is a wealthy trading republic because of where she sits." He gestured to the trees clinging to the cliffs. "These islands provide the perfect lair from which our intrepid ships can launch raids on theirs. Wealth must be shared."

Having been ridiculed for his former vocation, it would have been wiser for Kon not to disclose that the acquisition of wealth wasn't the reason he had chosen piracy, but his tongue got the better of him. "It's the slavery," he muttered as Drosik was in mid-throw.

The pebble hit the water with a plop and

sank. "What?"

Kon clenched his jaw. "I can't abide the notion of men, women and children being abducted from their homeland and deprived of freedom."

Drosik sneered. "You're a lunatic."

Kon stared out at the rippling waves, resolved not to utter a word of his dreadful experience at the slave market in Bari during the imperial occupation. His impulsive attempt to free a kidnapped woman had resulted in a severe beating at the hands of turbaned slavers and disciplinary action by his commanding officer. "Mayhap you're right."

Drosik clamped a bony hand on his shoulder. "On the morrow we sail to Venezia to scout out our next prize. We'll need extra crew. You seem like an honest man to me, if a little mad. Welcome aboard."

Kon shook his head at the irony. He'd been judged an honest man by a pirate, and mayhap the eccentric fellow was right about the madness too. He sent another stone bounding across the water, then followed his new captain to the cog lying at anchor in the shelter of the hidden bay.

MISTRESS OF THE FLEET

Polani Apartments, Venezia

"My pompous uncle Pietro is Doge of Venezia, yet I was not selected to sit on his council of *sapientes*," Zara Polani hissed, pacing the elaborately tiled floor of her family's private apartments adjacent to the Doge's chapel, the Basilica di San Marco. She crossed her arms tightly. "I cannot be an *advisor*, despite the fact I own a fleet of the most successful trading ships in the republic."

Smiling too sweetly, Ottavia looked up from her sewing. "However, dear sister, in the eyes of Venetian law, Bruno owns the fleet."

It was a lamentable truth. Their father had been legally obliged to bequeath his fortune to his eldest son, though her beloved brother was an imbecile. It didn't make her younger sister's retort any easier to bear. She ought to be immune to the pointed reminder by now. "But everyone is aware Bruno is a twenty-five-year-old child and I am the one in charge. They insult me because I am a mere woman. Who

5

better to advise the Doge on the constant threat from neighboring city-states anxious to sink their teeth into our wealth? Genoa, Pisa, they are no better than the Dalmatian pirates."

Seated in a well-upholstered chair by the cold hearth, Ottavia paused in her needlework. "Ugh! Pirates."

Zara rolled her eyes. Ottavia had inherited their mother's passive and sometimes sarcastic nature, whereas she was her shrewd father's daughter in every way. Given his son's mental state, he'd passed on to Zara his intimate knowledge of the trading routes that had made their family wealthy. She'd sailed with him as far as Byzantium and relished every minute—the storms, the tides, the waves, the sheer beauty and power of the sea. Ottavia had never set foot on a ship, but she enjoyed the fruits of the fleet's success, the coin, the exotic spices and perfumes, and of course the silk fashions.

Zara preferred male attire for her daily inspections of their ships docked in Venezia's lagoon. She lived by her father's mantra—an absentee *mercante* wasn't likely to prosper. Experience had taught her that seafaring men paid no heed to orders issued by a woman in a frock.

Confronting her uncle regarding the insult would be a waste of time since he wasn't happy having an advisory council of *wisemen* forced on him in the first place. He'd also made no secret of his resentment when it became evident his older brother hadn't bequeathed the Polani fleet to him.

Determined not to allow the trembling fury to control her, she sat down, toed off her satin slippers and pulled on her boots. "How do I look?" she asked, getting to her feet.

Ottavia didn't approve of the Tuscan wool leggings, knee high boots and tight fitting tunic carefully tailored to minimize her inconvenient breasts. Her sister wrinkled her pert nose. "Like a pirate."

Pleased with the response, Zara braced her hands on her hips. She would tend to what was important and let the powerful men of Venezia flounder in their own incompetence. "I'm off to the docks," she declared, though her first stop would be the family chapel in the basilica. The Polani fleet couldn't have prospered over the years without the help of the Almighty and she sought divine protection at every opportunity.

She exited the opulent apartment and set off with her waiting armed escort for the basilica and thence to the lagoon where her ships lay at anchor. She'd put reliable men in charge of loading the salt and woollen goods her captains would trade in the east for silk and spices.

However, it never hurt to keep a close eye on matters, especially when they were engaged in the distasteful business of transporting slaves for the Egyptian Fatimids who sold them in the market at Bari.

Rumor and suspicion were always rife among sailors, and the docks were a good place to glean intelligence concerning possible threats from sea raiders. She made jests about piracy, but it was the biggest threat to her future.

THE DOCKS

The brisk wind filled the square sail of Drosik's cog for most of the two-day voyage to Venezia, for which Kon was grateful. The brief periods when rowing was necessary tested his mettle, though he considered he was fit and strong. He developed a new appreciation for the endurance of his Viking ancestors.

By the time they rowed the *Ragusa* into Venezia's humid lagoon, every member of the crew had stripped off his shirt. Kon twitched his nose as sweat obscured his vision. Muscles he'd apparently never used before groaned.

He had a notion to give thanks to the Almighty that he'd been spared the agony of seasickness, but then remembered he no longer believed in God.

The extensive Venetian docks were abuzz with feverish activity. He had never seen hundreds of vessels anchored in one place, never heard so many different tongues spoken at once. Certain from early childhood of his vocation to the religious life, he'd always been keenly interested in the study of languages. He recognised Greek, Italian, Polish and his native German. Long lines of grimy, sweating men carried bales of cloth, barrels, rope, sacks of salt, weapons, and all manner of goods onto the waiting ships. It reminded him of anthills he and his brothers used to poke sticks at for the fun of watching the industrious insects scurry here and there.

His gut tightened when he caught sight of several turbaned Fatimids, their faces hidden. It confirmed his belief slaves were being loaded somewhere amid the hubbub. Bitter memories surged, and he feared for the captives.

Assured the *Ragusa* was securely moored, Drosik gathered his crew in the center of the hull, urging them to hunker close together. "We are here to gather information," he warned, "not to draw attention."

Kon deemed the caution amusing. Nothing drew the eye like Drosik's shirt.

"Wander around, pick out the ships loading the best cargoes and find out without raising suspicion when they expect to sail. I will make a pretence of seeking a cargo of our own. Wolf, you come with me."

The captain had congratulated himself at the nickname he'd bestowed, and Kon preferred it to the use of his family's noble name. It had become obvious during the short voyage that the pirate crew depended on each other to weather the many hardships of their occupation. It was vital for his survival he not be considered an outsider.

It occurred to him to grab his shirt before going ashore, but the others climbed over the side without bothering, so he did the same, imitating the captain's confident swagger as they progressed along the busy dock.

He slowed his pace when they passed the largest and most elaborately decorated cog. Gold embellishments adorned many parts of the sides and railings. Unlike the one masted vessels, another spar stuck out over the bow, perhaps for a smaller sail.

But what caught his eye and caused his heart to race was the stunningly beautiful woman standing with legs braced and hands on hips atop a platform at the front of the ship.

~ ~ ~

Zara had learned from her father the importance of keeping a watchful eye on foreign vessels docking in the lagoon. Some brazen pirates had been known to sail into Venezia precisely to scout out their next victim.

It was no easy task. The port teemed with trading vessels from the four corners of the earth from London to the Baltic, from the

North Sea to Byzantium.

She watched the new arrivals from the forecastle of the *Nunziata*, the flagship named for her late mother. An unfamiliar cog snared her attention.

The garishly dressed seaman in the bright red shirt who swaggered off the vessel must be the captain, but he held her gaze for only a moment or two.

It was the tall sailor following in his wake who intrigued her. He dwarfed his captain and was likely nothing more than an ordinary seaman, well-muscled, stripped to the waist and sweating. Yet there was something about his bearing, the set of his shoulders, the long, chestnut brown hair neatly tied back. He was swarthy, but she'd wager not Venetian. Men who spent any length of time toiling in the shipping trade had a lean, mean and hungry look. This man was more like a disciplined soldier than a pirate. She had little doubt the captain was a Dalmatian pirate. The reek of greed filled the air when he strode by, his all-seeing eyes on the goods being loaded onto her ship.

The fascinating sailor also looked across at the *Nunziata*. She became uncomfortably hot and gripped the railing of the forecastle when she realized he wasn't staring at the ship, but at her, his mouth agape. It wasn't the first time a man had been taken aback by her male attire, but when an amused smile lit up his handsome face a peculiar sense of recognition tightened her throat. Yet she was certain she'd never seen him before. She would have remembered such a man. Intrigued by a common sailor, a foreigner! Ottavia would be outraged!

Searching for an escape from his penetrating gaze, she looked away when three Fatimids appeared, herding a dozen or so chained captives destined for the market in Bari. She clenched her jaw, dismayed to see a young boy among the prisoners clad in ragged kaftans, though they were too light-skinned to be Arabs. However, at least this time there were no women. Slave-mongers were never to be trusted, especially ones who kept their faces hidden. It was a repugnant part of trade, but if Polani ships didn't transport the wretches, somebody else would.

When she turned back to the dock a few minutes later, Red-Shirt had walked on, but his crewman glared at her angrily, fists clenched, nostrils flared. His obvious fury left her strangely bereft. She wondered what had happened to change his demeanor, and why it mattered.

HATCHING A PLAN

Confused by the mixed emotions the striking woman had caused to swirl in his heart, Kon hurried after Drosik. Yet he was certain of what must be done. "I've found the ship," he declared breathlessly.

His captain eyed him curiously, then scanned the busy docks. "Which one?"

"With the high platform front and rear, and the mast over the bow."

Drosik scratched his armpit and chuckled. "The fore and stern castles, you mean. See how the railing is made to look like the turret of a castle? The front mast is for an *antemon.*"

Kon frowned at the unfamiliar word.

"A *headsail,*" Drosik explained patiently. "Makes it easier to keep a steady course. You have a good nose for booty! The *Nunziata* is a ship of the Polani fleet. Or was it Zara Polani who caught your attention? She's a beauty, eh? Mayhap you were right not to become a priest."

The hackles rose on Kon's nape. He couldn't deny the scandalously clad brunette had stirred his male interest, but his baser instincts had been roused years ago by the sight of the naked slave girl in Bari. That youthful folly had turned out to be a disaster.

He'd renounced the religious life, but he'd also sworn never to lust after a woman again. It inevitably led to heartache. Even his happily married father had been devastated by the loss of his wife. "I'm not interested in women," he assured his captain. "But I have an idea how to capture the *Nunziata*."

Drosik winked. "Best not tell the lads you don't like women, Wolf. They might think..."

Kon's gut lurched. He'd known men in the imperial army who were drawn to other men, and they'd been shunned, or worse. He searched for a plausible explanation. "It's not that I don't like women, it's...er...a religious belief, an oath."

Drosik shrugged, seemingly satisfied by this ludicrous notion. "Ever the priest, eh? What's the plan?"

Kon tried to gather his scattered thoughts. "I will get hired onto the crew of the *Nunziata* and ensure the ship is disabled when you attack."

It was a tenuous plan at best and he had no notion how he might sabotage a ship under sail without jeopardizing those aboard. There wasn't much point trying to save the slaves if they drowned.

"Brilliant," his captain exclaimed, but then he frowned. "And what do you want in return for putting yourself in harm's way?"

Kon didn't hesitate. "A guarantee the slaves will be released into my hands."

Drosik spat into his weathered palm and clasped Kon's hand. "Agreed, but watch out for Zara. She's a vixen."

His curiosity piqued, Kon wanted to know more. "It's considered bad luck for a woman to be aboard a ship. I'm surprised her father allows it."

"Father's dead. She has an older brother, but he's an imbecile. She runs the whole fleet. One of the more prosperous."

Now he understood the male attire. It must be difficult for a woman to garner the respect of sailors, but she'd evidently done so, and he admired her for it.

But she was a slave trader, and he couldn't allow the chained men being herded onto her ship to be delivered to market.

It was probable she'd do everything in her power to thwart his plot if she became aware of it, but he deemed it unlikely a woman would be aboard the ship when it sailed.

~ ~ ~

A loud argument at the far end of the dock

reached Zara's ears over the usual din of the port. Brawls were common, but she was surprised to see the Dalmatian pirate and his crewman pushing and shoving each other. She was too far away to glean the reason for the altercation, but pitied the puny captain if it came to a serious exchange of blows.

She should have been paying more attention to the loading, but the disagreement fascinated her. When the younger man raised his huge fists, the captain backed off and walked away in high dudgeon. Strange, but then who wouldn't be intimidated by the impressive muscles?

Her heart raced when the giant turned and strode towards her ship. Surely he wasn't... didn't expect...

She clenched her hands at her sides when he came to a halt on the dock below and looked up. His broad smile sent tiny winged creatures fluttering in her belly. "Are you hiring sailors? I'm strong and I will work hard."

As she'd suspected, he wasn't Venetian. The accent, Germanic she'd guess, only enhanced the deep timbre of his voice. She forced a reply from her parched throat, nodding in the direction of the now distant red shirt. "But you fight with men you are supposed to obey."

His eyes widened, but the smile remained. "He's a cheat. Refused to pay me. You strike me as an honest captain."

For a man to readily believe she was in command of the *Nunziata* sent pride rushing through her veins, though an inner voice cautioned he was merely using flattery. "Every sailor knows women don't captain ships," she replied. She sounded too coy for her own liking, but it was strangely thrilling to spar with him. She sensed he was no ordinary seaman, more like a man of breeding down on his luck perhaps.

His smile turned into a grin. "Can I apply to the real captain, then?"

Every man who frequented the Venetian docks and valued his life and livelihood knew enough not to toy with Zara Polani, yet she rose willingly to the bait and matched his grin with a sly smile. "I will inform the *real* captain you are hired."

He scaled the gangplank with agile ease, took the steps of the forecastle two at a time, went down on one knee before her and reached for her hand. His actions caused other members of the crew to move to her aid, but strangely, she wasn't afraid and waved them off.

"My thanks," he said, brushing a kiss across her knuckles. "You won't regret it."

She relished the warmth of his lips, preening like a queen fawned upon by a handsome courtier. She squelched the tiny nagging worry that she may have made a serious mistake.

~ ~ ~

Inhaling some unknown fragrance lingering on Zara Polani's skin, Kon looked up into eyes as green as emeralds and deeply regretted the blatant lie. But surely a lie uttered in order to save others from a terrible fate was forgivable? Still, lying was against his nature. Perhaps there was a little of the god-fearing Kon left, deep down.

Eyes fixed on the long, slender legs sheathed in male leggings and high boots, he had an insane urge to smother the elegant hand he held with kisses, mayhap suck a finger into his mouth. She'd deem him a pervert and have him thrown into the sea. And what in the name of all the saints had happened to his determination to ignore the temptations of the flesh?

"Your name?"

Her sultry voice sent gooseflesh marching up his spine. "Kon...Konrad," he stammered. "Wolf. Konrad Wolf, but everyone calls me Kon."

She slowly extricated her hand from his grasp. "Welcome aboard, Kon."

His name on her lips was a blessing. As he got to his feet, his mind filled with absurd images of lying abed with her, naked, being *welcomed aboard* as he thrust into…

Enough!

"Wolves are dangerous beasts."

He flared his nostrils and puffed out his chest. "*Ja*, it's short for…" Sanity returned. "It's a Saxon name. An unpronounceable mouthful. You wouldn't understand."

The emeralds darkened, then she averted her gaze to a tall man striding towards them. "Here comes *Capitano* Lupomari now. You will take your orders from him."

He watched her descend the gangplank, beguiled by the sway of her hips and the leggings clinging to her shapely bottom. The last time he'd seen wool of such fine quality…

The plaintive keening of the child chained beneath the stern-castle reached his ears and strengthened his resolve.

Zara Polani was his enemy, and best he not forget it.

NIGHT

Kon labored most of the day under the blazing sun, loading what he was instructed to load, and stowing it where he was told to stow it. It was heavy and dirty work, but after a while he fell into the rhythm.

Zara Polani failed to reappear. He should have been relieved but instead was disappointed. He supposed she had other priorities to attend to and likely hadn't given him a second thought. Why the notion bothered him was perplexing.

He risked an occasional glance at the three armed Fatimids guarding the languishing captives. Their dark, unfathomable eyes only stared into nothingness and he imagined mouths twisted in sneering distrust behind their face wraps. The desolate memory of the enslaved woman he'd tried to free and the subsequent beating and humiliation he'd suffered in Bari twisted his gut.

He learned from a fellow crewman the captain was pushing them hard because the ship was due to sail on the early morning tide.

It was dark by the time they'd covered the cargo with animal skins and Lupomari declared the loading finished. Kon eagerly accepted the tumbler of liquid he was issued to quench his thirst. He gulped it down, discovering to his dismay it was watered wine of dubious vintage. He'd known he had no tolerance for spirits since suffering the after-effects of over-imbibing at Johann's wedding years ago.

Using the excuse of retrieving his only shirt from the *Ragusa*, he walked along the dock feeling light-headed and bumped into his pirate captain. Drosik grabbed his arm. "Are you drunk, Wolf?"

Kon shook his head. "No. I drank wine too quickly after spending hours in the sun. I'll be fine. We sail on the morning tide."

"I'd best get the *Ragusa* underway then. What's your course?"

Kon had only conjecture to go on. "Bari, I think."

Drosik rubbed his chin. "You'll hug the coast of Italy in that case. I know the ideal place to launch our surprise attack. Damaging the rudder will be the best way for you to disable the ship."

Kon's previous experience with sailing was plying the oars of a small rowboat on the Elbe with the help of one brother or another. He was fairly certain of where the rudder was, but as for disabling it? "I'll figure it out," he promised, wishing he was as confident as he tried to sound.

The Lord would help him.

He cursed inwardly, exasperated that his thoughts still drifted heavenward. There would be no divine intervention since God didn't exist. Success depended on him alone.

He walked purposefully back along the dock, boarded the *Nunziata* and found a spot among the other snoring crew members sprawled in the hull. Still thirsty, he toyed with the idea of offering to bring water to the slaves, but the Fatimid guards would never allow him near their precious cargo. He covered his ears, tucked his knees to his chest and surrendered to exhaustion.

~~~

Zara stared up at the high ceiling of her chamber. Even in the darkness the gold leaf embellishments glowed. Too hot, she kicked off the fine linen sheets and let out a long slow breath of frustration. Try as she might to drift into sleep, the handsome Saxon kept surfacing in her thoughts.

Wolf.

He claimed it was short for his real name, but

what might it be? His bearing set him apart from any common sailor. His Italian was charmingly accented, but he spoke her language with ease and was obviously educated. He wasn't a man of the sea. Why did he want to work aboard her ship? It was hard to believe he might be a pirate, but had he truly abandoned the Dalmatian?

She tried to imagine what her father would think of him, but came to the strange realization he would have taken a liking to Konrad Wolf.

It was bothersome.

Resigned to a sleepless night, she got out of the big bed and called her maid to help her prepare for the coming day. "Tell the guard to summon my escort," she told the yawning girl when she arrived. "I am going to the docks."

"But it is still dark, *mia signora*," Flavia protested.

"*Tuttavia*," she insisted. "I will go *nevertheless*, after I pray in the chapel."

~~~

For years, the march south from Termoli to Bari with the imperial army had haunted Kon's dreams and it seemed tonight on board the *Nunziata* would be no different. He became restless as the memory of miles and miles of dusty roads once again disturbed his sleep and

24

he tumbled into the familiar nightmare.

But suddenly, the dream changed and he was marching in water up to his neck but couldn't make headway. Duke Heinrich's sneering face surfaced out of the waves, berating him for setting a bad example by drowning in front of his men.

A ship emerged out of a thick fog, carved on its prow the figurehead of a golden goddess. She sang an alluring siren's song. "I can save you from the depths of loneliness and despair."

"Help me," he pleaded. "I must get back to the Elbe."

She held out an elegant hand. "Who calls to me? Who are you?"

"If only I knew," he choked in reply.

The ship sailed on into the mist and he was once again marching to Bari and the inevitable destiny awaiting him in the slave market.

FIGUREHEAD

It was still dark when Kon was prodded awake.
He bumped his head hard on a rowing thwart as
he scrambled to his feet. A millet biscuit was
thrust into one hand, a mug of ale into the
other. Ravenous, he bit into the biscuit and
nigh on broke his teeth.

Sniggering laughter greeted his grunt of pain.
"Dip it in the ale," someone yelled.

He followed the suggestion and managed to
chew and swallow the resulting tasteless mush.
Rubbing his bruised head, he sipped the ale,
but was soon obliged to guzzle it down when all
hands were summoned to grab a pole and help
shove off.

Flickering torches left on the docks by the
night-watch cast an eerie glow on the confusion
as men scurried here and there, responding to
Lupomari's barked commands. The captain
wanted to outpace other ships which were
apparently preparing to leave on the tide. Kon
wondered if the *Ragusa* was among them. The
captives had only spent one night aboard the

vessel, yet the stink of human misery emanating from beneath the stern-castle was pungent, overpowering the usual nauseating reek of the docks.

Dawn in the Venetian lagoon stood in sharp contrast to his youth in Saxony when his beloved mother's voice had roused him and his siblings out of their comfortable beds. A lifetime ago. He could never go back.

Pushed into a rowing thwart, he flexed his stiff fingers before gripping the rough wood of the oar. This was the reality of his life now. The *Nunziata* was a much bigger cog than Drosik's. Rowing her out of the lagoon would take the combined effort of twenty men and he'd be expected to do his part.

When the order came, he gritted his teeth and pulled hard, strengthened by the resolve to free the wretches languishing in their own filth.

Amid the grunts of toiling men, the splash of oars, the creak of wood on wood, the eventual flapping of the unfurled sails, it came to him there was something unusual about the voice calling the command to pull.

As the wind toyed with the mainsail, he turned on the thwart to face the forecastle. An icy hand gripped his gut when he beheld Zara Polani. Her face was in shadow but he felt her gaze on him. Then she turned, lifted her chin and was transformed into a living figurehead etched against the rising sun, proudly guiding her ship into the unpredictable waters of the Adriatic Sea. She was the embodiment of the siren goddess of his dream.

Guilt and confusion gnawed at him. Had Zara joined the voyage because she suspected he intended to rob her of the ship she obviously loved? If the dream foretold true and she was the one who might save him from his despair, he cursed the fate that had made them enemies.

~ ~ ~

Zara relished the glow of the rising sun on her face, but a chill lay across her nape. She gripped the railing, determined to be rid of the wanton sensations rippling through her body as she watched Wolf heave on the oars, the muscles of his broad back tensed beneath the thin shirt.

She was drawn to a man she didn't trust. She hadn't intended to join the voyage, but an insistent inner voice she couldn't silence forced her to be aboard the *Nunziata* when the ship sailed.

She'd been wooed by many handsome men, the majority interested only in the Polani fortune and the power it brought. None appealed, until now. But Wolf wasn't a suitor, only an ordinary seaman—except she knew in her heart he was much more.

She inhaled deeply, filling her lungs with the salty air she loved, glad of a respite from the stench at the rear of the ship. Four days to Bari and they'd be rid of the slaves and their loathsome keepers.

Long days afloat with Kon Wolf loomed like a giant rock she'd have to steer clear of—an impossibility. Perhaps she'd cut him loose in Bari. Keeping an eye on his activities without wanting to get to know him threatened to be exhausting.

She whirled round, sensing a presence though she'd heard no one approach. Such carelessness at sea could prove deadly, especially for a woman. Her heart raced when she set eyes on Kon.

He effected a courtly bow. "Forgive me, *Signora* Polani, it was not my intention to startle you."

She raked windblown hair off her face, struck again by his manners and educated speech. "I wasn't startled," she lied. "And it's *Signorina* Polani."

She clenched her fists, perplexed she had deemed it necessary to tell him she had no husband.

His eyes smiled, but his jaw remained

clenched. "I request permission to remedy the wretched conditions the slaves are forced to endure."

Unreasonable disappointment pricked. He'd come to talk about the slaves. Zara the blushing virgin turned quickly back into Zara the shrewd woman of commerce. "I am aware of their plight, but the Fatimids will not allow any of us near their wretched cargo."

He frowned. "But you own this ship. Surely they will obey."

She held up a hand to silence him. "I can do nothing. In four days they will be offloaded at Bari and you won't have to worry on their account any longer."

Anger blazed in his blue eyes. Taken aback by the unexpected vehemence in his gaze she gripped the railing behind her. She stopped breathing when he leaned towards her, his mouth inches from hers.

"I wanted to tell you how beautiful you are, but slavery is a sin against God."

He turned on his heel and jumped down the steps into the hull.

Fury at his mutinous behavior warred with a longing to hear his deep voice whispering of her beauty. The confining tunic was suddenly too tight. No man had ever been foolhardy enough to criticize her. She looked to the stern-castle and wished she had the courage to challenge the Fatimids. But they paid handsomely for space aboard Polani ships and there were many in Venezia who stood ready to steal the business.

~ ~ ~

Kon fisted his hands and brought them down hard on the wood of the wale, determined to ignore the mocking voice in his head. But the memory of Zara's enticing lips refused to leave him.

You should have kissed her while you had the chance.

He'd probably alienated her completely and would most likely be told to leave the crew, or thrown overboard for mutiny.

The inability to hide his feelings concerning slavery had landed him in trouble before, yet he seemed incapable of containing the indignation seething in his throat.

Now along had come the added complication of Zara Polani and her tempting body. Why did she refuse to acknowledge the atrocity being perpetrated under her nose?

But he recognised he shouldn't blame her. She was a woman who'd survived and prospered in a man's world, and success in trade often depended on turning a blind eye.

He admired her though he despised what she stood for.

If he still believed in God, he might think he was being tested.

"Job von Wolfenberg," he whispered to the wind, then shook his head at the selfishness of the notion. His trials were paltry compared to the captive child and his compatriots. He simply had to learn to have the patience of Job and not betray his emotions.

BODYGUARD

The *Nunziata* was a well-built vessel, yet a surprising amount of seawater managed to seep through the tarred moss used for caulking under the wooden laths.

Kon and two others were assigned the job of bailing out the water by means of a bucket passed from one man to the next and dumped overboard. It seemed an easy task until he'd spent over an hour doing it under a blazing hot sun. His hands were blistered and he had a raging thirst.

"This ship isn't as sturdy as I thought," he panted to the other three.

One beamed a toothless grin. "Isn't too bad. Most ships are worse. Only two more hours and we get victuals."

Two hours!

Scooping up more seawater, he gritted his teeth. His lot was easy compared to the horrors the slaves must have suffered since being taken from their homeland. At least he was free to come and go as he pleased. He suspected from

33

their language the captives might be from Croatia. It was of some consolation there were no women among them, but the boy couldn't be more than seven or eight. The likelihood he would be sold into the Mamluk slave armies of Egypt churned his gut.

He avoided looking over in their direction, afraid he might be tempted to once again cause a ruckus, one he wouldn't survive. His dagger was no match for the curved *scimitars* the Fatimids carried on their hips.

Zara stayed on the forecastle, but had several animated conversations with Lupomari. It was impossible not to hear his name mentioned and it was clear they were arguing over the slaves. Perhaps their plight was of concern to her.

He worried about the route they were taking. Zara had confirmed they were headed for Bari, which meant they were hugging the Italian coast, far from the islands of Dalmatia. "Where will we drop anchor tonight?" he enquired of his comrade.

The man licked his lips and swiped the back of a filthy hand across his brow as he scanned the horizon. "Polani ships often stop in the bay at Scardovari."

He was none the wiser and simply had to hope Drosik did know the trade routes well enough to intercept them. His people had been pirates in the Adriatic for hundreds of years.

They were eventually given food. The salted pork filled his belly but aggravated his thirst, hence he guzzled the ale, knowing he'd regret it later. He discovered something in the millet biscuits he hadn't noticed in the pre-dawn darkness. They teemed with weevils.

His belly rebelled. He offered his to another deckhand who grabbed it eagerly. "Weevils is the only fresh meat you'll get," his comrade jested.

For the afternoon watch he was assigned to various tasks from learning how to repair ropes, to keeping an eye out for tears in the sail, to scrubbing the planking with holystones. As they worked their way from stem to stern, he fervently hoped he wouldn't be required to scour the area occupied by the slaves. The Fatimids brandished swords when they got too close, urging them away.

Daylight was waning when Lupomari guided the flat-bottomed *Nunziata* into the shelter of what Kon assumed was Scardovari Bay. To his surprise the captain pulled him away from the scrubbing gang. "You've worked hard this day," he said gruffly. "I'm assigning you to *Signorina* Polani's bodyguard. You're not to let her out of your sight while she is ashore."

While it was preferable to smoothing splinters

out of wood with stones, he wondered how *Signorina Polani* felt about Lupomari choosing him. He looked up at the forecastle. The slight inclination of Zara's head and the trace of a smile indicated that the captain perhaps hadn't been the one to choose him.

~~~

It was folly to appoint a stranger she was attracted to as one of her guards, but Zara reasoned it was the best way to keep an eye on him.

She'd watched him as the afternoon progressed. No matter what he was doing his attention was never off the slaves for long.

He'd smiled broadly when the child fell asleep in the arms of a man she assumed was his father. The depth of his caring for these unfortunates touched her heart, but it was troubling. He seemed to be obsessed with their plight and she hoped he didn't intend to do anything rash.

Fate had dealt the captives a cruel blow, but if it was God's will...

She shook her head, unwilling to accept such inhumanity as part of God's design. The sleeping child should be playing in a field full of flowers somewhere. His mother must be frantic at his loss. She'd never given much thought to motherhood, nor to the devastating effects the kidnapping of breadwinners and children must have on the women left behind.

Preoccupied, she watched the sun slowly sinking and again failed to hear Wolf's approach. She was startled when he spoke.

"I'm to be your escort."

A ludicrous image sprang up behind her eyes —she and Konrad Wolf parading arm in arm into the Doge's palace, dressed in fine raiment, the envy of all.

She lifted her chin, cursing herself for a fool. "Lead on then, Wolf."

Smiling, he offered his hand and led her down the steps of the forecastle, then helped her over the side into the shallows.

"Over there," she said, pointing to an area of the cove she knew would provide protection from the elements.

She was glad of the strength of Wolf's hand as they made their way across the pebbled beach. His solicitous behavior confirmed her belief he was no ordinary seaman. She perched on a rock, intending to ease off her wet boots as two of the crew brought kindling and lit a fire. "Where are you from?"

Wolf toed off his boots. The breath hitched in her throat when he hunkered down in front of her, and helped pull off the reluctant boots while he watched the flames cling to life in the light breeze. It was the most intimate thing any man had ever done for her, yet he seemed to expect nothing in return.

"I told you. Saxony."

"You are no sailor," she replied as he set her boots to dry.

Even in the twilight his eyes betrayed a wistful longing. "Wolfenberg is far from the sea." But then he clenched his jaw and watched her wiggle her toes in front of the fledgling fire. He was the first man to see her bare feet—a daunting and exhilarating notion.

She feared she might be pushing him to reveal more than he wanted to. "You're Wolf from Wolfenberg?"

"It's a long story," he muttered, gazing into the flames once more.

"We have the whole night."

She instantly regretted the suggestive words.

He glanced at her toes again but made no remark, confirming her suspicion he was a gentleman.

Suddenly he got to his feet and picked up several pebbles. "Can you skim stones?" he asked.

IMPERFECTIONS

A cherished memory of her beloved father warmed Zara's heart. "I was good at skimming when I was a child."

He grinned, walking gingerly across the pebbles barefoot. "That sounds like a challenge."

Never one to back down from a dare, Zara laughed. "Perhaps it is, but you'll have to carry me to the sand."

Her sister would be appalled at her behavior, but Ottavia was in Venezia, whereas she was on a beach watching the moon rise with an intriguing man who was both serious and playful. What harm in giving rein to feelings suppressed for too long for the sake of the family business?

Wolf looked back at her bare feet. "Ah, of course. A gentleman would have realized." He threw his cache of stones to the sand then scooped her into his embrace and cradled her against his chest. She slid her arms around his neck and giggled when he exaggerated the discomfort of walking on pebbles to the sand. When was the last time she'd giggled like a girl?

She inhaled deeply, filling her lungs with the warm zephyr. Surrendering to his strength was a momentous step, yet she felt freer than she had in years. When he set her on her feet and moved away to gather up stones she wanted to wail like a spoiled child.

Perplexed as to what had become of Zara the ruthless, independent woman of business, she embarked on the search for her own arsenal.

"The secret is in the shape," he shouted.

"Thin and light," she agreed, recalling her father's advice.

He returned to her side, brows arched. "I'm impressed. My record is seven skips, what's yours?"

"Six," she lied, having once achieved eight, much to her father's delight.

He drew back his arm, ready to throw. "My sister, Sophia, can do eight. It's astonishing."

His words irked her. "Why? Because she's a woman?"

He shrugged. "No. Because she's my sister, and brothers don't like to be bested by sisters, especially younger ones."

She laughed heartily. "I wouldn't know, I have no..."

Then she sobered, mortified by what she'd

almost blurted out. Bruno might be an imbecile but he was her flesh and blood.

Wolf's stone skipped five times before sinking. He wrinkled his nose in an endearing way she'd noticed before. Somehow it was safe to reveal the truth to him. "I have an older brother, Bruno, but he is...he cannot..."

He came to stand facing her, opened his hands to reveal the stones in his palms. "Each one of these is perfect in its own way, but some are skimmers and others are not. It doesn't mean they are good for nothing. Some are simply pleasing to look at." He poked one with pits marring its surface. "You might be of the opinion this ugly thing won't work well, but I'll wager it will fly the farthest over the water precisely because of the imperfections."

He turned to the water, bent his knees, leaned back and threw the pitted stone.

He counted the skips out loud, the rising excitement in his voice infectious. She laughed with joy for him when he thrust his hands in the air and strutted like a rooster after it splashed eight times. "*Ja!* A new standard for Konrad von Wolfenberg."

She was overwhelmed by conflicting emotions. His sudden frown betrayed his regret at the disclosure of his true name, but the nobility in his simple words had freed her from a lifetime of confusion regarding Bruno. "You are right. I haven't appreciated my brother's strengths. He is still a child in many ways, innocent and trusting."

He came to her and brushed a calloused thumb across the tear trickling down her cheek. "If only everyone was that way."

"I haven't trusted anyone for a long time," she admitted, drawn into the depths of his blue eyes, "but I have faith in you."

The warm breeze turned chilly when he averted his gaze. "You know nothing about me, Zara."

~ ~ ~

She trusted him! The lying scoundrel who intended to rob her of all she held dear. He had an urge to fall at her feet and beg forgiveness for his duplicity.

But his regret wasn't solely that he was no longer his father's son. He was plotting to rain devastation on a woman he was drawn to in a way he'd never experienced. He admired her spirit, the things she'd achieved, and he craved her body, despite his resolve to control his male urges.

And he'd once aspired to a life of celibacy!

She had wandered off and was throwing stones into the water, but in a half-hearted way. He regretted he'd disappointed her, failed to respond to the trust she'd admitted to placing in him. He sensed she wasn't a woman who confided in others. Perhaps if he told her a little of himself...

He growled out the painful truth. "I was supposed to become a priest."

She didn't take her eyes off the water. "Most younger sons end up taking the path of religion."

"No. I wanted to be ordained. I had a true vocation."

She glanced at him. "You would have made a good priest. You care deeply about people."

He snorted. "Problem is, I no longer believe in God."

Such an admission would result in his arrest in many places, and he marveled he had told her the truth. A burden had been lifted from his shoulders, but when he betrayed her she would question his sincerity. He was relieved when Lupomari arrived in the clearing, accompanied by the cook, both carrying food that smelled temptingly like...

"The men have netted a bounty," the captain cried. "Sardines!"

FLOODGATE

Lupomari brought good news as well as sustenance. "I persuaded the Fatimids to allow the slaves to bathe in the sea, but not before they forced them to clean up the filth."

Zara hoped the tidings would bring a smile to Kon's face, but he merely grunted as he perched on a rock and ate his meal.

She finished her portion of the roasted fish, babbling about how much she loved sardines. She couldn't get her thoughts off Kon's assertion he had lost his faith.

The captain had proven his worth time and again. In normal circumstances she enjoyed discussing the voyage, the ship, the crew, the weather; but this night she willed him to leave, filled with a compulsion to challenge Kon.

Lupomari picked at his food nervously as if he sensed her reluctance to respond to any of his efforts to begin a conversation. He finished his sardines and stiffly declared his intention to ensure the night watch was in position.

There were many things she wanted to say,

but once her captain had left she didn't know where to begin. A dreadful premonition that whatever she said would change both their lives seemed to have rendered her mute. As a faithful adherent of the Church, she should condemn him, but she was unaware of the reasons for the dire change in his beliefs. If she pried too hard...

After long minutes he got up, collected the discarded fish-heads and tails and threw them into the flames. "Rats," he muttered.

She murmured her understanding.

He walked across the pebbles to the water and knelt to wash his hands in the rippling waves. He wiped them on his shirt then retrieved her boots and brought them to her. "Should be dry by now. Better not to sleep barefoot."

She obeyed as he dropped more wood on the fire then sat to put on his own boots.

Hoping her judgement hadn't failed, she got up and went to sit beside him. He moved over slightly and leaned forward, resting his forearms on his thighs. She pressed her hip against him, taking courage from his solid strength. She inhaled deeply then put her hand on his broad back. It was the most daring contact she'd ever initiated with a man and the heat of his body flooded her veins. As longing spiralled into her womb, she prayed desperately that her words wouldn't alienate him. "I am an excellent judge of character, Konrad von Wolfenberg. You are a good man. You may have turned your back on God, but He hasn't abandoned you."

He tossed a tiny sliver of driftwood into the flames. "If only it were true," he whispered.

~ ~ ~

As if he needed more proof of his worthlessness, Kon's *rute* was insisting forcefully he should simply have his way with the woman pressed against him. Her warmth, the scent of the sea that clung to her, the gentle caress of her hand rubbing his back, all conspired to fill him with longing. He was about to rob her of her ship, why not her maidenhead?

But such a travesty would entail the loss of his own virginity and the prospect held him back. He raked his windblown hair off his face and sat up straight. "I am a miserable sinner."

To his surprise, she chuckled. "How can you believe in sin if you don't believe in God?"

He was still searching for the answer when she meshed her fingers with his. "Tell me your story."

He looked into her emerald eyes and let the floodgate burst open.

He told her first of his part in the invasion of Italy by the imperial army.

"You were forced to be a soldier when you wanted to be a priest," she said softly, never letting go of his hand.

"Yes, but I was honored to do my duty, to represent my family and fight for my Emperor."

He told of the battle for Salerno, and the surrender of Termoli, then eventually of his outrage at the slave market after the army occupied Bari, and of his attempt to free the young girl.

"It was noble of you."

He shook his head. "Perhaps, but I lusted for her body."

After a long silence, she asked, "Was she the first female you'd seen naked?"

He gritted his teeth. "Yes, and I wanted her despite her degradation."

"You were young. Her beauty moved you."

He snorted. "In more ways than one, but I paid for my foolishness with a beating. She paid too, despite having done nothing. The only thing I achieved was more pain. The slavers branded her."

His gut churned at the hideous memory. Zara's fingers had turned white in his grip. "Duke Heinrich disciplined me in front of my men for causing a disturbance in the market when my responsibility was to keep the peace."

She startled. "Heinrich of Bavaria was your commander?"

"*Ja*. He's probably been elected Holy Roman Emperor by now. Lothair handed over the regalia to him before he died during our retreat from Italy."

She shook her head. "Heinrich is dead."

He must have misheard. "What?"

"Apparently, the Electors deemed him too proud to be emperor. The man they did elect, Conrad Staufen, stripped him of both his duchies. He was in the midst of fighting to get Bavaria back when he died unexpectedly."

Guilt surged. He wasn't sorry a man he hated was dead. "He was known as Henry the Proud, but how do you know this?"

"Venezia is the crossroads of the world. Not much happens we don't hear news of."

Something she had said echoed. "Conrad Staufen is the Emperor?"

"Yes."

Memories surfaced of his father's diplomatic dealings with the Staufens. "I don't know if my father is still alive," he muttered, swallowing hard. "He may have died while I've been away, no doubt bitterly disappointed in me."

"Where have you been that you're not aware of these events?"

"Wandering," he replied. "Trying to find... something, though I'm not sure what it is. After the avalanche in the Pale Mountains..."

"Avalanche?"

He told her of his head injury from the rockfall and the growing feeling of worthlessness on the long journey home.

She put her arm around him.

He inhaled deeply. "And then my mother died."

She leaned her head on his shoulder. "When I lost my mother I cried for sennights," she confided.

The swell of her breast against his back gave him courage to tell the worst part. "I loved my mother dearly, but I've never shed a tear over her death."

~ ~ ~

Zara sensed she was sitting next to a volcano on the verge of erupting. Kon trembled as whatever demons he held inside seethed to get out. It was humbling he'd shared a great deal with her, but his inability to cry over his mother's death had to be addressed. Perhaps he came from a stoic family who didn't let emotions show. "Did your brothers weep at your mother's funeral?"

"Buckets. Even Johann who is actually my half-brother, my father's son by a first marriage. He's probably Count von Wolfenberg by now."

Her suspicions had been correct. "Your father is a count? I sensed you were of noble blood."

He shook his head as he turned to look at her, his blue eyes full of pain. "I am so noble, my head is full of the notion of kissing you."

The certainty she was gazing into the eyes of her destiny sprang to life deep inside Zara's core and blossomed like an exotic flower inside her body. She wanted his kiss, longed for his touch. "There is nothing ignoble in that."

She trembled when he put his fingers under her chin and tilted her face. His lips brushed hers and the spark of desire ignited a fire within. She held her breath and traced her tongue over his lips, savoring the salt and something unique she'd never tasted before. The taste of a man. Her heart careened around her ribcage when he growled and deepened the kiss. It seemed natural to open her mouth to his coaxing tongue and suckle him.

He breathed his need into her, taking everything she gave, but giving of himself in return as he held her tightly in his strong arms. His lips were on her neck, one hand cupping her breast, his thumb brushing the nipple as he embraced her. It was wrong but very right at the same time. She had never allowed a man close, yet wasn't afraid. She lay her palm on his warm neck and let the astounding sensations of physical need take hold of her body, surprised to realize she was the one making the strange mewling sound.

He broke them apart and rested his forehead against hers. "I want more than a kiss," he rasped, taking hold of her hand.

Panic surged when he pressed her fingers to his hard maleness. She tried to withdraw, but he held firm. She wanted to join with him, but not on a beach, with her crew...

Suddenly, pebbles crunched as he fell to his knees and took hold of both her hands. "I have frightened you, and such wasn't my intent. You had to see how much I want you."

"I want you too," she murmured. "But..."

He put a finger to her lips. "Hush. I have a confession to make."

CONFESSIONS

Feeling the bite of the pebbles beneath his knees, Kon cursed himself for a fool. As usual, he was his own worst enemy. Having tasted Zara, filled his hand with her breast and felt her response to his touch, he recognized he could never endanger her life nor steal anything she held dear. Revealing the truth would likely toll the death knell for any relationship between them, but...

The flames of the dying fire flickered in her jewelled eyes and he resolved to hold her gaze while he bared his soul. "You should not put your trust in me, Zara. I am a pirate."

She tried to pull her hands away but he held fast. "I was sent as a spy by Drosik, the captain I was arguing with on the dock. It was a ruse to get me aboard your ship."

She stared, her lips pressed together in a tight line, her shoulders rigid. "You are nothing but a thief, then? A man who lies about being of noble birth? Will you rob me of my innocence as well?"

He shook his head. "My purpose in joining forces with Drosik was solely to rescue the captives."

Her mocking laughter took him by surprise. He eased his hold and she struggled to stand. "You are a fool to believe a man like Drosik would go along with such a plan. If you deliver my ship to him he will take everything, including the slaves."

He got to his feet. "But he has given me his word."

She braced her legs, fisted her hands on her hips and squared her shoulders. Her defiant stance emphasized the splendor of her breasts and only increased his need of her. "The word of a pirate?" she spat.

It hit him like a bolt of lightning. She was probably right. He'd been naive to trust Drosik. "I swear to you, I no longer intend to fulfill my part of the bargain with him."

"And why should I believe you?" she taunted.

He replied without hesitation. "Because I am drawn to you."

She glared at him with such vehemence that for a moment he feared she would call for the captain and have him clamped in irons, but then she slumped onto the rock where they had kissed and whispered, "And I to you."

~ ~ ~

Zara didn't want to need Kon's comforting embrace, yet when he sat beside her and gathered her into his arms, she sobbed against his chest. "You must be a priest," she lamented with a hiccup, "why else would I confess such a thing?"

"I have caused you pain," he murmured into her hair, "and I am heartily sorry. I will do everything in my power to protect you and your ship, but we must free the slaves."

She flattened her hands on his chest and pushed. "It's impossible. I understand your feelings regarding slavery. I've never been comfortable with the practice and I will undertake not to carry human cargo on Polani ships in the future. However, the Fatimids will kill you if you try to free these men."

He made no reply. His silence worried her as they clung together. She listened to the steady thud of his heart and wondered what he was thinking.

"You are tired," he said at last. "Let me wrap you in your blankets and bid you goodnight."

She let him lead her to the shelter of the rock where she'd slept on previous voyages, a safe haven discovered by her father. He tucked the blankets around her and pecked a kiss on her nose.

"Will you lie with me?" she whispered, sifting

her fingers through his soft hair.

He shook his head. "You are too tempting. I will keep watch."

Her emotions in knots, she watched him walk away until the darkness swallowed him up.

FOG

Lupomari emerged from the mist the following morning, carrying what looked like chunks of real bread. Kon's belly growled.

"All's well?" the captain enquired.

Propped against a large rock a few yards away from where Zara lay, he had watched her sleep fitfully, regretting he was the reason for her disquiet. "All's well," he replied, getting to his feet.

However, all wasn't well in his heart. He'd spent the night plotting scheme after scheme to free the captives without endangering Zara and the rest of the crew. She was right, it was impossible.

"Thick fog out on the water this morning," Lupomari told him. "I don't like it, but the lookouts haven't heard anything untoward."

Kon looked out at the impenetrable white blanket, hearing only the waves lapping at the rocks and the distant call of seagulls. "Will it clear?"

The captain shrugged. "Maybe, maybe not.

You'd best go claim your rations before everything is devoured."

It was understandable Lupomari considered him no better than a simple seaman but he was disappointed nevertheless not to be breaking bread with Zara. He wanted to assure her once again of his determination to thwart Drosik.

He waded into the shallows and climbed aboard. It was eerily quiet, the enveloping mist muffling every spoken word, every footfall. There was no creak of wood on wood as the cog sat motionless in the still air.

"Bad luck," a ship-mate growled.

Kon surveyed what was left of the rations and decided to forego the scraps of millet biscuits, hoping his belly would survive on the memory of the sardines from the previous night. He grabbed the last tankard of watered ale. "What is?" he asked in an effort to take his mind off his hunger.

The man pointed to the wall of white. "Creatures lurk out in the deeps, and how's a ship to avoid them if we can't see?"

Kon was slightly amused as he sipped the ale, though the man seemed genuinely agitated. "Creatures?"

"Servants of Satan, with arms longer than the mast of this cog and tentacles that can pluck a man right off a ship and drag him to his death."

Anxious to be sure Zara got aboard safely, Kon was relieved when she and Lupomari appeared on the forecastle.

Apparently, the captain had overheard. "No more superstitious nonsense," he shouted. "Prepare to weigh anchor."

The man scowled, then slunk off.

Kon was taking up an oar when Zara summoned him. He stood at the foot of the steps to the forecastle and looked up, desperate to erase the lines of worry marring her beauty.

"Wolf," she said without smiling. "It will be slow going this morning, a good opportunity to learn how the rudder is controlled. Go watch the steersman on the stern-castle."

He obeyed, his thoughts confused. Did she suspect his original intention to sabotage the rudder? It was doubtful, otherwise why send him there? Mayhap she wanted to spare him the prospect of more blisters on his already blighted hands. Nevertheless, he tasted the guilt tightening his throat.

On the stern-castle he'd have a better chance of watching for an opportunity to help the captives, if the mist ever cleared. It was a forlorn hope the Fatimids would drop their guard, and what if they did? He'd have to kill them and the chances of killing three...

He mounted the steps, relieved the stench

from below wasn't as bad as before. No doubt it would worsen as the day progressed.

He saluted the steersman known only as *Rospo*. With a triple chin, warted skin, huge eyes, toothless grin and short bandy legs, the man looked, moved and smelled like the pond creature he was named for. "I'm to learn from you," he said.

"Right," Rospo croaked.

Suspecting he'd get no more out of the fellow, Kon braced his legs, keeping a close eye on his mentor as the call came to pull at the oars and the cog lurched out of the bay, propelled by the oarsmen.

The captain and Zara were distant, blurred figures on the forecastle. Lupomari shouted commands as they made their way slowly to the open sea. Rospo echoed the orders and swung the tiller accordingly. He apparently had confidence in Lupomari. A quarter hour seemed like an eternity. Kon feared they'd run aground at any moment on the rocky shore. "I suppose the captain knows these waters well," he remarked when his nervous heart stopped racing.

Rospo shrugged. "Your turn."

Kon stepped up to the tiller, though his legs had turned to mush, and took hold, grateful Rospo didn't let go altogether. He gained confidence slowly as *steorbord*, and *larbord* became familiar terms. It was relatively simple. It also became alarmingly apparent how easy it would be to disable the rudder by damaging the tiller.

~ ~ ~

Weary of peering into the white fog, Zara looked back at the stern-castle, barely able to make out Kon and Rospo at the tiller. She had prayed long and hard as the night wore on and hoped she had chosen the right path in entrusting him with the important task of steering.

He'd sworn his loyalty to her and an inner voice whispered she had to trust him.

Nevertheless, there was no harm in ascertaining his progress from Rospo, though in five years she'd never been able to elicit more than one word responses from the gruff fellow.

Pulling tight the thong binding back her hair, she picked her way carefully past the rowing thwarts, elated to feel an unexpected breath of wind on her face. Lupomari shouted for the sail to be hoisted. Men eagerly began the task, voices raised as they pulled together, seemingly equally relieved that perhaps the worst was over. Her captain was skilled, but fog had sounded the death knell for more than one Venetian ship.

She mounted the steps to the stern-castle, delighted to see a broad smile on Kon's face. "You seem to be enjoying your new responsibility," she teased.

"As long as Rospo here keeps his hand on the tiller alongside mine, I'll be fine," he replied.

She arched a brow when Rospo grunted, apparently pleased with Kon's progress. She'd always loved the sea. In some inexplicable way, sharing the voyage with a man she was increasingly drawn to made it more pleasurable. She closed her eyes and tilted her face to the weak sun. "The fog might lift soon. Smooth sailing from here on."

Her belly lurched when strident cries arose from below. She blinked open her eyes and looked over the railing to where the slaves were held. Two of the Fatimid guards were struggling to wrench the screeching child out of the arms of his distraught father.

She understood only a smattering of the Arabic language but her blood ran cold when she recognised the word *Siraya*. She looked back at Kon. "Contagion," she breathed.

INTO THE DEPTHS

Kon let go of the tiller, confident Rospo would continue to steer the ship. He was concerned for Zara who had rushed down the steps to intervene in whatever was going on below.

If there was disease aboard the ship, it would spread rapidly. When he reached the deck, his heart stopped. Zara had one long leg astride the wale and was pulling desperately at the robes of a Fatimid who had the boy in his clutches, evidently intending to throw him overboard. She was screaming something unintelligible at the Arab.

With a manacle still clamped around one wrist, the child clawed at the face of his captor, whose turban had been knocked askew, covering his eyes. Terror seemed to have struck the boy dumb. The father shouted desperate pleas in some foreign tongue while another Fatimid menaced him with a curved sword. The rest of the slaves were on their feet, their faces full of terrified outrage. The crew stared, apparently unaware of the mainsail dangling loosely in the still air, despite grunted warnings from Rospo.

Lupomari's hoarse command snapped them into action. Two hurried to right the sail. The rest turned to the struggle going on beneath the stern-castle.

Kon was afraid for Zara and the threat the Fatimid posed to her. He drew his dagger and lunged at the infuriated Arab, yelling a loud war-cry. As his weapon sank into the man's flesh, the brute released his hold on the boy. Zara lunged to save the child. His heart pounding in his ears, Kon heaved the Fatimid's body out of his way and grasped hold of her shirt. The fabric ripped and she and the boy tumbled into the sea.

He was vaguely aware of a melee in the cog's stern, but had no time to worry about the slaves now. The only thing that mattered was saving Zara. He hurriedly pulled off his boots, climbed onto the side and jumped.

~ ~ ~

Zara loved the sea, but she'd never experienced the numbing terror of falling overboard. The boy was ripped from her arms by the impact. When she resurfaced, gasping for breath, there was no sign of him. She cursed the ignorance of the Arab who had condemned the child for no good reason.

She was a strong swimmer. Her father had insisted she learn and she thanked him for it now. The *Nunziata* had drifted on into the lingering mist but Lupomari would drop anchor and come to her rescue. Muffled shouts from the direction of the ship confirmed it. The boots were making it difficult to tread water, but she thanked her patron saint for the male attire. Skirts would have dragged her to her death.

She took a deep breath and slipped beneath the surface, searching the clear water for any sign of the child, panic setting in when she found none.

Lungs bursting, she broke the surface, surprised to be suddenly in Kon's grip.

"Thank God," he gasped.

She struggled for breath, relieved to rely on his strength. "I can't find the boy."

He raked her hair from her face. "Mayhap it's for the best if he is deathly ill."

She shook her head. "Yellow eyes," she panted. "*Jalnice*. Not contagious."

"Can you stay afloat while I look for him?"

She nodded, and he was gone before she had a chance to deter him. If he drowned…

~ ~ ~

Kon had barely recovered from the shock of plunging into the deep water when Zara broke the surface. His immediate reaction was to offer thanks to the Almighty for her safe delivery into his arms.

Perhaps there was a God after all.

When she told him of the reason for the boy's ordeal, he knew he had to try to find him.

He filled his lungs and peered into the bottomless depths. The salt burned his eyes, and he acknowledged with a sinking heart that diving in the Adriatic wasn't going to be anything like retrieving rocks from the bed of the Elbe.

He struck out, kicking hard.

~ ~ ~

Zara's strength was fading, her arms on fire, her heart in knots. Despite the warmth of the water, a chill had seized her. No help had come from the strangely quiet and still mist-shrouded *Nunziata*. Something was wrong. And where was Kon? He'd been underwater too long.

She cried out her relief and consequently swallowed seawater when he resurfaced at long last. He had the boy tucked under one arm. "You saved him," she coughed.

He reached out his free hand to buoy her up, but his reddened eyes were bleak. "I was too late," he panted. "The lad drowned."

NEVER TRUST A PIRATE

"We must get back to the ship," Kon said hoarsely, spitting out seawater. "You're cold."

"I don't understand why they didn't come to our aid," she gasped as they swam in the direction of the *Nunziata*.

"I'm concerned the Fatimids may have gone berserk after my attack," he admitted.

"But it's too quiet."

As the hull loomed out of the mist, Kon spotted three bodies floating in the water. Given the turbans and robes, they couldn't be anything but Fatimids. "Mayhap I am wrong," he quipped when Zara gaped, her emerald eyes filled with alarm at the macabre discovery.

He was relieved when a rope ladder came tumbling over the side. He made sure Zara had a firm hold and was out of danger before hoisting the boy over his shoulder and beginning the ascent behind her.

Once on the deck, she reached up to hold the body while he climbed aboard.

He raked his wet hair off his burning eyes,

then took the child from her, befuddled that the crew seemed to have disappeared. The captives cowered in the center of the cog, all still chained, except the father of the boy. A second manacle dangled from the one around his wrist. He stared at the corpse, fists clenched, his distorted face wet with tears.

"Where is everyone?" Kon said, trying to fathom how chained men had done away with three armed Fatimids, the captain, and his entire crew.

"Loading the spoils onto my ship."

They spun around to see Drosik, grinning broadly, hands on hips, one foot braced on the wale.

Zara gasped in outrage.

Kon's gut knotted when he realized the Narentine's smaller cog was nestled alongside.

Drosik jumped down onto a rowing thwart. "Well done, priest. You delivered the *Nunziata* as promised."

"This is none of my doing," he growled, avoiding Zara's accusing gaze.

The pirate captain's laughter came to an abrupt halt when the boy's father bellowed like a wounded beast. He wrenched his son's body from Kon's arms, shoving him hard in the process and leapt over the side into the sea.

It happened so quickly there was no chance

to react. Kon staggered to regain his balance then ran to peer over the side. The wretch had disappeared into the depths. Nausea swept over him. He'd failed to save father and son from a terrible fate— but at least the rest would be free.

Drosik smirked. "Forget him. One less slave won't make much difference to my profit."

An icy hand gripped Kon's innards as Zara seethed at his side. "But you swore to deliver them to me."

Drosik wiggled his eyebrows and jumped back onto his own vessel.

"I warned you not to take the word of a pirate," Zara hissed.

~ ~ ~

Prior to sailing away, Drosik deemed it highly amusing to rope Kon and Zara together back to back. Anger throbbed in her aching head. "He's not going to get away with this. There's a dagger in my boot."

She leaned back against Kon. They were still soaked to the skin, but the warmth of his body had driven away the chill, along with the fury flooding her veins.

The rest of the crew were tied up in various parts of the cog. The slaves, the bales of cloth, the sacks of salt and the rest of the precious cargo were gone. All that remained were a few oddments of canvas and some of the hides used to protect the goods from the elements.

Kon expressed his regret over and over for what had happened.

She struggled with her anger. Someone had to take the blame, but she should perhaps have been more cautious. Ultimately any misfortune that befell a ship was the responsibility of the master. "You are not solely to blame," she finally reassured him. "It was a litany of errors. We're fortunate he didn't kill us and steal the ship."

"Not enough men to crew her," Lupomari shouted from somewhere nearby. "We're too big to be of use to a pirate."

Zara twisted and turned, trying to get a hand loose, but both wrists were tightly bound. "We have to get the weapon and cut the rope. He already has a head start."

"Push against me, and we'll try to stand," Kon suggested.

She was glad he hadn't argued, evidently understanding her desire for revenge.

Pressing back to back and bracing their legs, they managed to stand.

"Now, turn to face me," he said, "and I'll do the same."

It took several long minutes of straining already tired muscles for them to come together, face to face, her breasts pressed against his chest. It wasn't how she had imagined such a suggestive position coming about.

Then he smiled and her heart raced. Despite the predicament she allowed her body to melt into his.

"You are the most beautiful woman I have ever known," he said softly, pressing his hips against her.

She closed her eyes and pursed her lips, longing for his reassuring kiss.

Suddenly the rope loosened and fell to the planking. She blinked. Rospo stood beside her, levering the point of a dagger under the rope around her wrists, his big eyes dwarfed only by his wide, toothless grin.

Kon gaped. "You have a…"

"Dagger."

"How did you..?"

Rospo cocked his head towards the water. "Hid."

"Over the side?" Zara asked in disbelief.

"Rudder."

The resourceful fellow sprang off to free others while she and Kon stared. "He must have jumped in when they boarded and clung to the wood like a limpet," she said, kicking away the coils of rope.

"Mayhap Limpet should be his new name," Kon quipped.

She laughed, amazed that in the midst of despair and turmoil she still could. "I don't advise you try it."

He snaked his arms around her waist. "You seem to be enjoying this."

She clasped his forearms and inhaled deeply. "There's wind to fill the sail, my crew has a fire in their bellies, I've a fine ship beneath my feet, and a courageous man by my side. What more do I need?"

"Mayhap the weapons from the drowned Fatimids?"

"Good idea," she replied. "If Rospo hasn't already thought of it."

Lupomari regained the forecastle. "All hands to your stations. Anchor aweigh. We've a pirate to catch."

A SIGN

Hours later, Kon left the tiller in Rospo's capable hands and obeyed Zara's summons to meet by one of the rowing benches.

"We must plot our revenge carefully," she said as he joined her and Lupomari.

Kon was frustrated with what seemed to be slow progress. "Can we not go faster?"

"We don't want to catch him in the open sea. He'll simply out-manoeuvre us," Lupomari explained.

Zara nodded. "Or throw the cargo overboard and flee."

Kon tempered his impatience. "What's the plan?"

Zara unfurled a chart and lay it atop the bench, one end tucked under an oar. "My guess is he will sell off some of the booty before proceeding to Bari with the captives. He'll need coin to buy provisions and his crew will demand more money—selling slaves in Bari's market is a risky venture when you're not an established trader. The Fatimids guard their monopoly."

Kon pointed to the chart. "Ravenna would be the next port."

Zara shook her head. "He won't go there. It's a Papal State and they take a dim view of piracy." She traced her finger along the chart. "Cervia is unlikely since they produce their own salt. Two powerful families control Rimini and he won't want to tangle with them."

"Ancona, then?"

"Doubtful," Lupomari replied, scratching his beard. "The Anconian Republic has strong trade routes with Dalmatia and they sell more than they buy. Drosik is probably well known to them and they too don't tolerate pirates. Bad for business."

An eerie certainty crept into Kon's belly when he examined the chart further. "Termoli?"

Zara poked the map. "It would be my guess."

Lupomari took the chart and rolled it up. "Mine too. I propose we increase our speed and plan to arrive before him."

"Agreed."

Kon put a hand on the railing and swallowed the lump in his throat as memories assailed him. "I know the town. I was an officer in the imperial army that occupied Termoli during the invasion." Then he smiled when another thought dawned. "My brother, Lute, married a woman he met in Termoli, Francesca di Cammarata."

Zara frowned. "I heard tell of Ruggero of Sicilia's niece marrying a Saxon count. He's your brother?"

"Yes. Emperor Lothair endowed him with lands not far from Wolfenberg as a reward for his services. However, what's more important, Francesca had a maid from Termoli. Zitella left with her mistress."

Lupomari chuckled. "Must have been a man involved."

"You're right, but Zitella's family probably still lives in Termoli. Her father might be of help to us."

Zara pecked a gleeful kiss on his cheek. "This is a sign. God is with us. Set a course for Termoli."

The prospect of revisiting the coastal town churned Kon's innards, but it suddenly struck him like a blow from Thor's hammer that it was indeed God's will he go there. It was the last place he'd been Konrad von Wolfenberg, capable imperial soldier, aspiring priest and son of a prominent Saxon noble. His life had fallen apart after he'd marched south to Bari.

He'd been reborn and was once again in divine hands. Or mayhap he always had been and hadn't realized it. Was Zara right that his

Savior hadn't abandoned him? He would never be a priest, but renewed pride and honor surged in his veins. What's more, he had found a beautiful and courageous woman who would make a perfect wife.

~ ~ ~

Mixed emotions swirled in Zara's heart as her beloved cog skimmed the waves. Polani ships had lost cargoes to pirates before, but she couldn't recall a single instance when they'd pursued the thieves. There were always other cargoes. Her father's philosophy!

Drosik hadn't taken the *Nunziata*, hadn't murdered any of her crew. Why was she bound and determined to get back what had been stolen?

Frequent glances at Kon Wolf manning the tiller, legs resolutely braced, provided the answer. Salt, rope and cloth were replaceable. This was about rescuing and freeing the captives. It had taken a man who doubted the existence of God to open her eyes to the evils of slave trading—she, a devout Christian. She shuddered at the thought that had she not met Kon she might not have tried to save the boy.

Perhaps she was pursuing Drosik in order to avenge the man she was falling in love with. The pirate had taken advantage of his trusting nature.

She rejoiced that, by some miracle, the terrible events seemed to have rekindled Kon's faith, and she sensed he both dreaded and anticipated going to Termoli.

A troubling notion intruded. If he rediscovered his faith he might turn again to the religious life. She made the sign of her Savior across her body. God would surely strike her dead if she stood in the way of a man becoming a priest.

NIGHT AT SEA

In deeper water and with the aid of the stars, the *Nunziata* sailed through the night with Zara and Lupomari taking turns on the forecastle so no time was lost at anchor. Rospo manned the tiller for the captain.

With the slaves gone, and the wood scrubbed clean, a piece of canvas was stretched across the area beneath the stern-castle for Zara's privacy. The hides made a more comfortable bed than the bare planking. She had slept aboard ship before, and didn't fear the crew, but after several hours on watch she couldn't settle knowing Kon was close by.

As if sensing her need of him, he came to the shelter. "Are you asleep?" he whispered.

"No. Enter."

He knelt by her side, pulling one of the skins over her legs. "It's important to keep warm."

She couldn't see his face clearly in the darkness, but knew how tiring it was to spend hours at the tiller. It was the first time he'd taken on the task at night when winds might change unexpectedly. She cupped her hand to his cold cheek. "You must be exhausted."

He pressed his hand against hers. "You too. I wanted to make sure you were comfortable before I slept." He leaned forward to brush a kiss on her lips.

She wanted to respond, but was afraid she might be leading astray a man whom God had called to His service. He must have sensed her hesitation. "Sorry. You're tired."

She was a forthright person. There was no point hiding her fears. She sat up. "No. You have a vocation to be a priest. I couldn't bear..."

His mouth took possession of hers with a passion that robbed her of breath. There was no choice but to allow his tongue to enter and mate with hers, no choice but to let him breathe for her as his hand cupped her breast.

A moan of longing surged in her throat, but Rospo was only a few feet above them, the sleeping crew not far away.

When they broke apart, he nuzzled her ear. "I will never be a priest, Zara. It is you I worship, you I wish to serve. When this is over I want you for wife."

Zara's father had introduced her to many carefully selected gentlemen, every one eligible, wealthy, handsome. Some had offered for her hand. She'd supposed one day the right man would come along, but hadn't foreseen a proposal of marriage on a dark night aboard a ship headed into danger.

Despite her misgivings that she was thwarting God's plan, the answer came readily. "I will wed with you, Kon Wolf."

He kissed her gently then, but the brush of his thumb over her nipple sparked a fire in her loins. She lifted the blanket. "Stay with me," she murmured in a sultry voice she barely recognized.

He lay down and gathered her into his arms. "I want you, but I frightened you the last time I..."

"I'm not afraid now," she replied, pressing her hand to his hard maleness.

"You should be."

~ ~ ~

Kon had never burned with desire for a woman. The lustful episode with the slave girl was nothing compared to the fire consuming him for Zara. But he also craved her trust, her love. "I hope you can see my grin in the darkness," he teased, fearing he had alarmed her.

She traced a fingertip along his lip. "You make me feel things I have never felt before."

He nibbled her finger. "It's the same for me,

but joining our bodies now isn't what I want. Well, I want it, but it's not the right time or place. Our first union will be in a sweet smelling bed, and you will be my sweet smelling wife!"

She nuzzled her nose into his neck and lay one leg across his thigh. "But I ache."

"You are a temptress."

She thrust her breasts against him. "Touch my nipple again."

He lay her down and suckled one nipple then the other through the fabric of her shirt, thrilled when they pebbled readily beneath his tongue. She clamped her hand over her mouth and writhed, lifting her hips.

"I can relieve the ache," he rasped, suspecting she didn't understand what he had in mind, or how apprehensive he was. It was impossible to serve in an army without overhearing men boast of where women loved to be touched, but he also had his father's advice to fall back on. The von Wolfenberg children had benefitted from their liberal parents' insistence they be prepared to give pleasure in the marriage bed. Assuming as a priest he wouldn't need the knowledge, he wished now he'd paid more attention.

He moved his hand to between her legs, grateful for the male leggings she wore. He pressed against the warmth of her most intimate part and her hips quickly matched the rhythm of his touch. Sensing she was close to release, he covered her mouth with his. His heart rejoiced when she growled her ecstasy into his throat.

Minutes later, her body went limp, then she curled into him. "I never knew," she whispered.

His need was great, but his resolve greater. He thanked God for this woman who was his future, his Holy Grail, the meaning he had been seeking. "Some day I will touch you without leggings between us."

She purred her contentment and he suspected she would soon be asleep. "Although," he quipped, "I foresee a day when more women will wear such attire."

There was no response.

~ ~ ~

It was still dark when Kon shook her awake. "I'll go before dawn breaks."

She raised up on her elbows, still half asleep. "Why?"

"Well..."

"Kon, my beloved, we are on a ship. The *Nunziata* may be a large cog, but I can guarantee there isn't a man aboard who isn't aware you spent the night here with me."

"You don't mind?"

She yawned. "They know better than to

censure Zara Polani. I pay their wages, and besides, we are betrothed, aren't we?"

He kissed her lovingly. "And I want to shout it to the world."

"Not here, but perhaps you should relieve Rospo."

He stood and stretched his arms high over his head, making her wish she was still safe in his embrace.

She too stretched like a cat after he left. Now she'd known ecstasy she wanted more of it. But then the memory of her dream surfaced.

You're a temptress!

Mayhap without meaning to, Kon had given voice to her sin. His kiss and his touch had turned her into a wanton who'd encouraged him to break his resolve.

She'd been born with a strong will. It had made the difference in the survival of her family business, but perhaps her strength would prove to be her weakness.

LUST

Now he'd found what he believed to be the key to his happiness, Kon couldn't get enough of Zara. He watched her every move during the day. Rospo took him to task several times for not having his mind on the tiller when the wind shifted abeam. The man was never outwardly friendly, but Kon sensed a new edge to his abrupt nature.

Despite a determination not to spend the second night at sea in Zara's makeshift shelter, he was soon cuddling with her. "We must be more circumspect," he whispered, even as his mouth latched onto a nipple and suckled.

She pulled open her shirt and held her breast to his lips, sifting her fingers through his hair. "But I crave your touch."

Urged on by her throaty moans, he pulled the garment down to reveal both breasts. He gathered their bounty in his hands and feasted hungrily on both nipples.

Caught in the grip of desire he became vaguely aware she had lifted her bottom and was pushing the leggings off her hips.

"Touch me," she growled.

The aroma of female need assailed his nostrils, robbing him of willpower. He touched his fingertips to her woman's place. His *rute* rejoiced as her wet heat inflamed him further.

He savored her scent on his fingers and salivated for her juices. He came to his knees, clamped his arms around her thighs and lifted her to his mouth.

He couldn't name the taste—newly-baked bread, salty and sweet at the same time—but it sent his desire spiralling out of control.

She moaned and writhed and arched her back when her release came.

"Take me," she urged hoarsely.

He freed his *rute* from his leggings. She reached for him, gasping as she took hold of his rigid *manhood*.

He didn't want the first time to be like this, but...

"Rabbits!" Rospo growled from not far above them.

~ ~ ~

Zara lay absolutely still. Lust had rendered her witless. The strong-willed mistress of the fleet had become a wanton who had been willing to give away her maidenhead to a man she barely knew.

It was too dark to see Kon's face, but she sensed his frustration when he withdrew abruptly and staggered away from the siren who had come close to luring him to perdition.

She pulled up her leggings, covered her breasts and curled up, listening for other sounds of censure. Only the wind mocked the insistent throb of need.

She'd probably kept the men amused with her moaning. How was she to face them on the morrow?

Her father had drummed it into her that a *mercante* who lost the respect of his crew was destined to fail.

Had she affronted God and thereby doomed the expedition to rescue the slaves with her scandalous behavior?

~ ~ ~

Having no wish to face Rospo on the sterncastle, Kon sought refuge beneath one of the rowing thwarts, but still heard the sniggers.

His need of Zara had almost driven him to an act they would both regret. He cursed his *rute* that even now in the face of shame and self-loathing refused to be tamed.

He inadvertently touched his fingers to his nose. The lingering aroma of Zara further enraged the fiery dragon at his groin.

The bitter irony that he'd once aspired to be a

celibate only increased his turmoil.

He spent the rest of the night curled up under the bench, praying for divine forgiveness. He had come close to despoiling the virgin he was in love with.

He was a disgrace to the Wolfenberg name.

GIANLUCA

The *Nunziata* spent another day and night at sea before the square tower of Termoli castle came in sight. The squat, unimposing edifice evoked unpleasant memories for Kon. Lute had come close to being murdered atop those battlements. Emperor Lothair had suffered a seemingly minor flesh wound which subsequently putrified and led to his death.

Above all, Kon recalled the stifling heat of the town in high summer, which mercifully hadn't affected them yet out on the water.

The last hours aboard had been oppressive in a different way. Zara avoided him, clearly dismayed by the position he'd placed her in. Lupomari treated them both with cool disdain. Rospo croaked constant warnings about on-shore winds that might drive them aground.

Many of the crew barely concealed sly grins.

As dawn broke Lupomari guided the cog into Termoli's port.

"No sign of the *Ragusa*," Kon muttered to Rospo as the *Nunziata* nudged the dock. "Only fishing boats."

"*Sì,*" the steersman answered with a nod.

The captain summoned him to the forecastle. He was disappointed when Zara descended the steps and went in the opposite direction while he was still amidships.

"Do you see the man we seek, the girl's father?" Lupomari asked when he arrived.

Kon scanned the scores of fishing vessels and the several dozen men who swarmed everywhere, preparing to set out for the day's work. He'd only set eyes on Zitella's father once and feared he might not recognise him. "No, not yet."

"If we don't find him here, can you locate his dwelling?"

Kon had to rely on what Lute had told him of Zitella's family. "Yes, though I may have to ask for precise directions."

"Best you take Rospo with you. Your manner of speech will mark you as a foreigner."

"I will go with them."

Kon turned quickly, his spirits lifting when he saw Zara climbing the steps.

Lupomari bristled. "Not a good idea. This isn't Venezia."

"Who rules Termoli now?" Kon wondered aloud in an effort to fill the silence caused by Zara's glare.

"William," the captain replied. "But he is no longer Count of Loritello. Ruggero stripped him of the title when he retook the town."

"William will remember me," Kon said.

"Fondly?"

Kon shrugged. "He sided with the Emperor."

"We will take a contingent and explore," Zara declared.

Kon smiled, glad she seemed to have regained some of her aplomb.

"As you wish," Lupomari conceded.

When the cog was securely moored, Kon and Zara set out into the streets of Termoli with Rospo and two crewmen.

~ ~ ~

Zara wasn't hopeful they would locate the man they sought. Kon didn't know his name, only that his daughter was Zitella who had left with her mistress. There was no guarantee the fellow would help them. He might be resentful that his daughter had fallen in love with a squire in the imperial army, apparently the real reason she had followed Francesca.

The intention had been not to draw attention to Kon, but several curious youths soon gathered around. He must have recognised one and when he tapped his chest and said his name, they cheered. "*Commandante* Wolfenberg," they shouted. "Games on the beach."

Zara frowned in puzzlement.

Kon grinned. "My brother, Lute," he explained. "They remember him well. He organised games of ninepins for children during the siege. He wanted to keep them occupied and take their minds off the war."

"I wish I had met him," she replied, reminded once again of the nobility of Kon's bloodline.

The youths pushed and shoved to be the first to lead them to Gianluca Merluzzo's dwelling, buzzing with excitement over the good news of Zitella's marriage to Drogo.

It warmed her heart to see how readily Kon made friends with these young men. He had an openness that put them at ease. She understood. He'd quickly won her affection, yet the intense feelings that resurfaced every time she laid eyes on him had caused her to censure him.

As they approached, Gianluca staggered out of his modest dwelling. Zara suspected the hubbub had woken him and wondered why he wasn't out fishing.

The youths chattered at once, anxious to pass on the good news concerning his daughter. He quickly joined in the celebratory mood, ushering the visitors into his home. He bowed repeatedly when Kon informed him she was the niece of the Doge of Venezia and apologized over and again for the hovel in which he lived. She politely declined an invitation to sit on the only chair, fearing she might end up with splinters in her bottom.

The conversation eventually came around to the reason for their sojourn in Termoli. Gianluca listened wide-eyed, hacking up phlegm and spitting with disgust when told of the slave child's drowning. The spittle settled atop a dark mound on the dirt floor. He'd evidently perfected his aim over the years.

"We surmise Drosik will come here to sell or trade some of the goods before he heads for the slave market in Bari," Kon explained.

Gianluca hit the spittle mound again, without taking aim. "The pirate captain of the *Ragusa* is well known here as a cheat. It won't be hard to find folk to aid us."

The youths echoed his sentiments, all seemingly willing to participate and offering suggestions at once.

Gianluca silenced the cacophony with an impatient growl and another well-aimed glob of spittle. "First step is to make him believe we are agents for William who want to buy salt. Once aboard, we inspect, we argue, we decline, we leave, but we have discovered mayhap the best way to free the captives, how many men remain with him, where he has chained the slaves."

The youths accepted the plan enthusiastically, but Kon was sceptical. "He'll get suspicious."

Gianluca shrugged. "He is always suspicious. It's in his nature. You have a better idea?"

~ ~ ~

Kon had grave misgivings. "But as soon as Drosik sees the *Nunziata*, he will flee to a different port."

"We can cover the name," Zara suggested.

"You've seen the docks," Gianluca said. "There are at least a dozen large cogs. It's the reason I no longer fish. More to be earned by means of trade and barter, and less risky." He winked at Zara. "One day Termoli will rival Venezia."

She smiled indulgently. "I doubt it, but you make a good point, and if Drosik knows you as a trader, he'll be less suspicious."

Kon still wasn't convinced, but had no other plan to offer. "We don't have much time to prepare. Thank you, Gianluca."

To his surprise the fellow clamped meaty hands on his shoulders and looked him in the eye. "I thank God you and your army came to Termoli. My daughter has a better life with a good husband. I can never do enough to thank you."

It was a surprising revelation that Termolians

might consider the Saxons who'd invaded as benevolent, though the young lads certainly had an enduring fondness for Lute. His brother would be pleased when Kon told him. The realization that this was the first time he'd considered returning home to Saxony hit him like a blow to the belly.

He embraced Zitella's father, slapping him on the back, but had no words to offer in reply.

Zara too seemed moved by the simple man's gratitude and he was elated when she linked her arm in his as they made their way back to the port.

GREEN HAT

"My father must be turning over in his tomb,"
Zara lamented as she watched sweating
crewmen daub black pitch over the *Nunziata's*
name and the gold filigree along the wales and
railings of the stern and forecastles.

Rospo and another man were busy removing
the heavy spar over the bow, so the cog would
appear not to be equipped with a headsail. "He
assures me he can keep a steady course without
it," she told Kon nervously. "Hopefully we'll
have time to make repairs before we set sail
again."

The men were putting the finishing touches to
the changes when the lookout clinging to the
top of the center mast called out a warning of
Drosik's appearance at the entrance to the port.

Zara made the sign of her Savior. "Watch
over us, Lord," she prayed as they took up their
posts, "and forgive me, Papa."

Kon hunkered down next to where she sat in
the forecastle. His closeness gave her courage.
"I am sorry for the other night. My need of you

is so great, I lost control. However, I meant what I said. When this is over, you and I..."

She gently pressed a fingertip to his lips. "I am sorry too. I've tried hard to be an equal among men; I'm not used to being treated like a woman."

"You've had to be strong for the sake of your family," he reassured her, "but when you are my woman..."

His promise sent warmth flowing into private places.

"Hush," Lupomari hissed. "The thief is securing his cog, and here come your salt buyers."

Zara looked back to the town. True to his word, Gianluca was approaching the port with a small retinue of young men. He'd evidently bathed and changed into cleaner clothing. A tall green hat sat atop his head like an upside-down acorn. "He's enjoying this," she hissed.

"Let's hope he doesn't scare Drosik off by appearing too eager," Kon said.

"I have confidence in him," she confessed. "He's dealt with the pirate before. He'll know how to handle him."

~ ~ ~

Peering through the struts of the forecastle railing, Kon watched Zitella's father stroll onto the dock. He growled when the fool strutted past the *Ragusa* as if hadn't noticed the ship.

"What's amiss?" Zara hissed impatiently. "Drosik won't see me if…"

"No," Lupomari insisted. "You must remain hidden. It's too risky. If he spots you, all is lost."

Kon was exasperated. "Gianluca has walked right past the cog."

She chuckled. "Good. I told you he knows what he's doing. Drosik will come to him now."

Kon sneered when the red-shirted pirate strode onto the gangplank, put two fingers in his mouth and whistled. "You're right."

Few on the dock paid any attention.

Gianluca made a big pretence of trying to ascertain who was whistling, then walked towards the *Ragusa*.

"What's happening?" Zara asked.

"Looks like Drosik is boasting of his cargo."

Zara smiled. "Gianluca will pretend not to be interested."

"It's exactly what he's doing. Walking on. Drosik is following him along the dock, cajoling. The lads are playing their part too, trying to shove him away from Gianluca."

Kon's apprehension subsided a little. "Mayhap this ruse will work."

Despite his new confidence, his gut tightened again when Gianluca and his compatriots went aboard the *Ragusa*.

The men walked back and forth, huddled, then broke apart. Voices were raised, hands thrust in the air. The scene repeated itself again and again, the voices getting louder each time. He caught an occasional glimpse of Gianluca's peculiar green hat and the gaudy red shirt he'd come to hate the sight of.

Then suddenly there was silence. "I can't see anybody."

"Where have they gone?" Zara whispered.

Kon gritted his teeth. "I don't...Hold on... Gianluca is leaving the *Ragusa*. But where's his hat?"

Lupomari chuckled. "He's traded it."

"For what?" Zara muttered.

Kon had to smile. "I'd say for the sack of salt one of the lads is carrying on his shoulder."

Zara tried to get to her feet. "But the salt belongs to me. It's worth more than a stupid hat."

Kon put a hand on her arm. "Not to Drosik. He looks pleased with the deal. It's a good thing he has big ears, otherwise the hat would be over his eyes."

"Madonna," Zara exclaimed. "When I get my hands on him..."

"Patience," Kon urged. "His time will come. We'll wait a bit, then follow Gianluca."

~ ~ ~

Drosik strutted on his cog, shouting orders to his crew for what seemed to Zara like an eternity. "What is he doing?" she asked again, frustrated they couldn't leave to seek out Gianluca.

Kon had been hunkered down in the forecastle for too long. He'd given up and now sat beside her, rubbing his knees. He reached for her hand, but his frown was troubling. "I'm guessing he doesn't intend to leave the ship and his cargo. Mayhap the episode with Gianluca roused his suspicions."

Her dismay was tempered by the startling arrival of Rospo crawling up the steps.

"Boat," the steersman croaked, without opening his mouth.

It was both amusing and a mite worrisome. After five years she understood his meaning. "He's brought a boat alongside," she explained to Kon.

Bent double to avoid detection, they made their way down from the forecastle to the opposite side of the cog. Rospo kept a lookout as they slipped over the side and descended the rope ladder he'd secured.

"Resourceful fellow," Kon remarked, taking up the oars of the rowboat.

Zara looked up at the frog-like face peering

at them from the cog. "He's a strange little man but it's not the first time I've depended on his proven loyalty."

She pushed off against the *Nunziata* when Kon pulled on the oars. "It's as I said before," he reminded her, "you can't judge a person from outward appearances."

Then he chuckled.

"What's funny?"

"I sound like my father."

DEBTS

As they moved further away from the *Ragusa,* Kon had to concentrate on guiding the rowboat in and out between cogs and fishing vessels moored in the bustling port. Rowing on the Elbe didn't involve dodging other vessels and they experienced a few collisions.

He pondered his own words. He'd spent months wandering across Europe trying to rediscover who he was when the truth was obvious. He was Dieter von Wolfenberg's son, in fact as well as in name. He had inherited his father's compassion and consideration of others. If only he had the same patience and could learn to control his volatile impetuosity.

Once out of the port, he rowed with more confidence towards the beach, aided by an onshore wind. "During the invasion, we pitched camp along this stretch," he told Zara. "Brandt's lieutenant, Vidar, recommended we move away from the beach into the dunes. It proved to be good advice when the tide washed out some of the tents pitched in the shadow of the castle wall. Seems like only yesterday."

"It was before you were sent to Bari," Zara remarked, blurring his amusing memory of irate soldiers scrambling out of wet tents.

Wood scraping bottom echoed the emptiness in his gut. They jumped out of the boat and dragged it up on the deserted sands.

"Yes," he managed. "Lute and Brandt remained here. Johann and I went south."

They stowed the oars in the boat and began the long walk into the town.

"Now you are struggling to reconcile the proud Saxon who left Termoli with the man who lost himself in the slave market in Bari."

He took her hand. "You're too perceptive, *Signorina* Polani. I was, but you've helped me in my search. You've seen things in me I'd lost sight of."

"Your true nature shines through, Kon Wolf."

Her words warmed his heart, and though she didn't speak of love, he was confident she loved him.

~ ~ ~

It became evident during the brisk walk into the town that the folk they encountered were aware of Zara's identity. They bowed deferentially, the name *Polani* uttered loudly as they passed.

Kon smiled. "Judging by the wide-eyed shock at your attire, they don't approve, but your reputation keeps them silent."

"It's surprising. Our ships rarely dock in Termoli, yet they are aware of our fleet."

"I'd wager Gianluca hasn't kept his mouth shut about our presence here. Or mayhap his retinue of youths."

No sooner were the words out of his mouth when they were surrounded by those same young men, all talking at once, gesturing wildly.

"They're speaking too fast for me," Kon complained.

A worry gnawed at Zara. "They say the slaves weren't aboard the *Ragusa*."

He came to an abrupt halt, his weather-bronzed face ashen. "What?"

She pushed through the excited throng. "We must wait to hear what Gianluca has to say."

Zitella's father came out to the door and ushered them within, insisting the youths remain outside. The only change in the miserable place seemed to be the sack of salt stashed in one dark corner.

"You've heard? Definitely no captives aboard, unless he has them hidden under the thwarts. Impossible. You couldn't hide a dog in such a confined space."

"Surely he hasn't sold them already?" Kon asked, scratching his head.

A certainty crept into Zara's heart. "He's put

them ashore somewhere, under guard. Probably less risky than bringing them into port."

Gianluca nodded. "There did seem to be few crewmen aboard."

Zara pointed to the sack of salt. "Speaking of cargo, that belongs to me."

The Termolian shrugged. "It's mine now. I traded for it."

Zara clenched her fists at her sides. They were dependent on this man's goodwill, but business was business. "A hat!"

"You claimed you would do anything in gratitude for Zitella's happiness," Kon reminded him.

"But my debt is to your family, young man, not to *Signorina* Polani. In Venezia she is mistress. Termoli is my domain."

She recognised it was useless to argue. Better to play a waiting game. "Well then, great trader of Termoli, where has he put the captives ashore?"

"There are many places he may have chosen," Gianluca replied, brandishing an impatient fist when one of the lads poked his head in the door. "Be gone, Pio!"

"There is a man here," Pio explained nervously, clutching the battered door. "He claims to know where the slaves are."

~ ~ ~

Kon's first instinct was to dismiss the notion. Probably some local who'd heard of the situation and sought to take advantage.

But his father's face loomed. Dieter von Wolfenberg was always ready to hear what everyone had to say before rushing to judgement. "Bring him in," he said, overruling Gianluca's spluttered objections.

The bald man who stooped to enter the meagre dwelling wasn't what he expected. "You're not a fisherman," he charged.

The stern-faced stranger bowed to Zara, then stretched out both arms. "I suppose my splendid attire gave me away."

"Your manner of speech tells me you're not Italian either," Kon said.

"He's not from around here," Gianluca confirmed.

"Yet there's something familiar about you," Kon said, searching his memory.

A trace of a wry smile tugged at the corners of the man's mouth. "We have met before, but I wasn't as well dressed then."

Kon studied him. The shirt and leggings, though of fine quality, were a mite snug on the tall man's frame. "And these are not your garments."

"You are right. I regret I had to steal them."

Gianluca scoffed. "A thief!"

Zara folded her arms. "Enough of these riddles. Who are you?"

Kon's shoulders tensed when the fellow took hold of her hand and raised it to his lips.

"*Signorina* Polani, permit me to introduce myself. I am Jakov, Count of Istria, but you know me as the man whose son you risked your life to save."

RESURRECTION

Zara withdrew her hand quickly. "The slave? But your hair was long."

Jakov grimaced. "Had to shave it. Lice, I'm afraid. One of the unfortunate consequences of confinement in appalling conditions."

Kon stepped forward, confusion evident on his face. "I saw you drown."

"Such was my intention," Jakov admitted. "My son's death destroyed any will I had left to survive. However, the water filling my lungs aroused anger in my heart. If I surrendered to despair, the other wretches captured with me, loyal men in my army, would have no chance of rescue. I kissed my child farewell and gave his body up to the sea." He swallowed hard, plainly stricken by the cruel memory. "My desire for vengeance renewed my strength, though I barely made it to shore. I'm not ashamed to tell you I wept as I watched the pirate ship sail away."

"Army?" Kon asked.

"Istria is a beautiful part of Croatia, but its location at the end of a peninsula that juts into the Adriatic makes our more remote villages prone to raids by slavers. I maintain a small army to protect my people, but this time they took us by surprise. I must admit I never thought they would dare to attack a town as large as Pula and take me, and my son." He turned to Zara. "They were Venetians, by the way, lovely lady."

She had to sit on the rough stool she'd avoided before her trembling legs buckled. "It doesn't make sense. You were brought aboard by Fatimids."

"Your compatriots sold us in Venezia at the first opportunity. Quick profit."

Zara was still fighting disbelief. "And how did you get from Scardovari to here?"

Jakov sighed. "Alas, another theft. A horse. The pirate sailed close to shore. It was no great challenge to follow his progress. My spirits rose when I caught sight of your ship in pursuit."

Silence dominated the tiny dwelling.

"But you were chained," Kon said.

Jakov shoved back the sleeve of his shirt to reveal the ugly band of metal still clamped around his wrist. "I thank you both for your bravery in trying to save the life of a stranger's child. Vedran was my heir, but this manacle is his only legacy. I will wear it until the day every last one of my compatriots is free."

~ ~ ~

Kon grasped Jakov's hand. "I am elated you are alive. My sole purpose in sailing on the *Nunziata* was to secure the freedom of the captives before the ship reached Bari. I'm only sorry we couldn't save your child."

Jakov returned the handshake, but arched a brow. "I watched you during the voyage and I am more certain than ever you are no ordinary sailor."

"He's the son of a Saxon count," Zara replied with a smile and obvious pride that made him want to puff out his chest.

"Dieter von Wolfenberg," Kon explained when Jakov frowned.

"The diplomat?" the Croat asked. "The one who convinced the intractable Staufens to support Lothair's invasion of Italy?"

Kon supposed he shouldn't be surprised his father's stellar reputation as an imperial negotiator had reached as far as Croatia, but it filled him with a new sense of purpose. "He's the one, though it's a good while since I left Wolfenberg. He wasn't well and may have died in my absence."

Jakov shook his head. "Last I heard a month ago from the imperial court he was still alive."

Kon meet Zara's sympathetic gaze, and he sensed his eyes betrayed the longing to return home he'd refused to acknowledge before.

Gianluca coughed gruffly. "This resurrection is all well and good, but where are these confounded slaves?"

"Up the coast," Jakov declared. "Heavily guarded."

"Best we make haste," Zara said. "Drosik will set sail to retrieve them if he cannot sell his wares here."

Gianluca chuckled as he produced another hat from a sack on the dirt floor. It was identical to the green one he'd traded to Drosik, except it was nigh on the same garish shade of red as the hideous shirt. "I can delay him a while longer," he said.

~ ~ ~

An hour later, picking slivers out of her woollen leggings, Zara reluctantly agreed the plan was sound.

Gianluca would accompany her when she sought an audience with William of Loritello to formally complain that the *Ragusa* carried contraband stolen from the *Nunziata*. He was confident the reputation of the Polani fleet and his own influence would gain them a quick hearing.

Accompanied by officials, Zara and her captain and some of her crew would then board the *Ragusa* and keep Drosik pinned down in the port while the cargo was reclaimed.

Meanwhile Kon and Jakov would attack the guards holding the slaves a few leagues away.

She and Kon were the last to leave Gianluca's dwelling. He put his arms around her waist and kissed her tenderly. "All shall be well," he reassured her. "You will get back your goods and the captives will be freed."

Foreboding tightened her throat. "I would prefer to come with you. I have a terrible feeling I'll never see you again."

"Have faith," he whispered.

He kissed her again with deeper passion. She opened her mouth to allow his tongue entry, put her arms around his neck and pressed her body to his. She relished the brush of his soft beard on her face, savored his male taste, thrilled at the hard proof of his need.

She was elated he was on the path to rediscovering his faith, but terrified by the seed of doubt had taken root in her own heart.

THE BEST LAID PLANS

Zara, Rospo and Gianluca were ushered into the the musty and sparsely decorated hall of Termoli castle. Kon had described William of Loritello as a corpulent individual. The sagging double chins were an indication the gaunt-looking man who greeted them had at one time carried extra weight.

She supposed being stripped of a title by King Ruggero had been a harrowing experience, but at least the Sicilian hadn't chopped off William's head.

She was out of practice and he was no longer a count, but she deemed it wise to curtsey respectfully. "Thank you for granting an audience, my lord," she crooned.

Sprawled in an elaborately carved chair, he raked his eyes over her attire. "It is indeed a pleasure to welcome a member of the Polani family to our humble port."

Zara had met many like William in her uncle's far more opulent court in Venezia. Their cold words spoke one language, the heat in their gaze quite another. She was aware of his advances towards the woman who had eventually married Lute, but deemed it better not to mention the von Wolfenbergs.

"You bring a complaint?" William asked Gianluca, evidently deciding to deal with one of the males in the delegation.

Determined to assert her position, Zara replied. "There is a cog in your harbor, the *Ragusa*. Its cargo was stolen from my ship several days ago by its captain, a man named Drosik. I'd like it back."

She bit her bottom lip when William turned again to Gianluca, "Is this true?"

She gestured to Rospo. "This man will attest to what I say."

William steepled his fingers, tapped his chin and looked up into the rafters. "But he is in your employ, is he not? Why should we believe him?"

The accusatory nature of his question confirmed her opinion. She was dealing with a man who wields no real power but who likes to believe he does. She beckoned Rospo, who sprang forward and bowed politely.

"As a *Polani*," she stressed, "I can vouch for Rospo. He is an honest man and I humbly beg you consider his testimony accordingly."

William glanced at her sharply then his glare

faltered momentarily and she was satisfied the power of her family name had served its purpose. He addressed her for the first time. "He is called Rospo? Like the pond creature?"

She resisted the urge to smile. "Yes, my lord."

William shifted his weight and spoke to Rospo. "Can you confirm this charge? Drosik carries contraband stolen from your *mistress*?"

Rospo nodded. "*Sì.*"

William drummed his fingers on the carved arms of his chair. "Where did the theft take place?"

"Scardovari."

The puppet-ruler of Termoli clenched his jaw. "How did the alleged pirate manage to board your ship?"

"Mist."

William stared at Rospo as if he wasn't sure if he was being made a fool of. "What was stolen?"

"Salt."

The former count scoffed. "That's it?"

"Cloth."

Zara held her breath, hoping Rospo wouldn't mention the slaves. It would complicate matters if none were found aboard the *Ragusa*.

"Rope," he added.

William steepled his hands again and gnawed his fingernails. After an eternity he stood and announced, "We will deliver our decision in an hour."

Her heart lurched. Every minute wasted made it more likely Drosik would leave the port, but William waved them out before she could protest.

~ ~ ~

Jakov advised Kon they should go by foot to the river inlet north of Termoli where Drosik had offloaded the captives. "It's more than ten miles, but they'll easily spot us if we approach by boat. The coastal path is easy. Two of us will be able to tackle the guards."

Four hours later, he signalled a halt. "We should head inland from here and approach downriver. The land is too flat and open where my men are being held."

They eventually came to the river where they quenched their thirst then sat down in a leafy glade to rest and plan their strategy.

"Assuming they are still chained together, how will we free them?" Kon asked.

Jakov opened the satchel slung across his shoulder and produced an adze. "Another ill-gotten gain!" he confessed with a wry smile. "I used it to break the chain off my manacle and thought it might come in useful sometime."

"You're a resourceful man," Kon said.

"Needs must..." Jakov replied soberly.

Kon wondered briefly if he would have such steadfast courage were he ever placed in the same predicament. "What's the lay of the land?"

"The river is wider at its mouth, and lightly treed. The sun will be high in the sky in a little while. Chances are the guards will be dozing."

"How many?"

"Two, but well armed, and my fear is they may kill my men rather than surrender them."

"Drosik won't be happy with that notion."

"True. It's a risk we must take."

Kon had carried a *scimitar* across his back. Retrieved from the body of one of the drowned Fatimids, its intimidating curved blade shone in the bright sun when he lifted it over his head and brandished it. "Hopefully these Arabic weapons will put the fear of God into them."

Jakov patted the hilt of the *scimitar* Lupomari had given him. "Do you believe in God, Konrad?"

He hesitated. "Not long ago, I would have said no, but now…"

"Never abandon your faith, my friend," Jakov urged him. "I came close to losing mine when you carried my son's body back onto the ship, but it's only with God's help that I am here with you today."

Kon pondered his words as they followed the narrow river to its mouth.

~ ~ ~

Zara followed two of William's soldiers along the dock. "I can't wait to see Drosik's face," she crowed to Rospo. "You did well and I thank you."

She was surprised to see a blush spread over the warted features.

He left her as they passed the *Nunziata* in order to round up more of the crew. She and the soldiers carried on towards the *Ragusa*.

"Wait," Rospo shouted.

"We have the law on our side," she exclaimed confidently, increasing her pace. "Nothing he can do."

She reached the gangplank a moment before the first soldier and stalked aboard ahead of him. She shouted to the pirate. "Drosik, where are you hiding?"

He'd apparently been napping on the forecastle and sat bolt upright. She smirked when the green hat fell over his eyes. He tossed it away and scrambled down the steps. Members of his crew followed him as he rushed to challenge her. "Get off my ship," he screamed, his face as red as his shirt.

His glare faltered slightly when he espied the soldiers. "What's going on here?"

"Your vessel is carrying contraband," the soldier declared. "By order of William of

Loritello you are to return the goods to their rightful owner, Zara Polani."

Drosik's beady eyes darted here and there, but then he folded his arms and lifted his chin. Her confidence faltered at the wily smirk on his face. "Zara Polani does not have a right to claim my cargo. She is not the owner of the Polani fleet. Bruno Polani owns the ships and their cargoes, and therefore I am not obliged to give her anything."

Zara scoffed, but to her dismay the young soldier shot her a questioning look. "Is this true?"

"Yes," she had to confess, "but..."

"Then we can do nothing until we speak with our master."

Men and their stupid rules!

In disbelief, she watched them regain the dock and march off. She turned back to Drosik, only to discover he'd rushed to the forecastle. His crew had retrieved the poles and were ready to shove off.

Desperate, she peered along the dock. Lupomari and Rospo were leading men from her ship. She had to delay the pirate or all was lost. Side-stepping the rowing thwarts, she hurried to the stern-castle, intending to wrest the tiller from the steersman.

In her panic, she didn't notice one of the

rowers had thrust an oar into her path until it was too late. She fell forward heavily, banging her forehead on the planking. Dizzy, she sat up, clutching her throbbing head. Her fingers came away wet. Staring in confusion at the blood on her hand, she heard the sounds of running feet, shouts of protest, but the familiar movement beneath her meant the cog was already underway.

~ ~ ~

As Jakov had predicted, Drosik's men were sleeping in the shade of the leafy trees when he and Kon crept close to the clearing. The captives also appeared to be asleep, but stirred when Jakov made a strange sound. "They'll recognise the call of the red-throated loon," he explained. "It's a common sight in Croatia and a signal we often use."

To Kon it sounded more like a tomcat seeking a mate, but it had produced the desired result so he kept his opinion to himself.

The captives sat up; one returned the bird call.

Perhaps the clinking of chains woke one of the guards. Suddenly, he was on his feet, heading toward the captives. Jakov sprang out of hiding with a blood-curdling yell and swiped his blade across the fellow's chest. The pirate crumpled to the ground, his dagger still sheathed at his waist.

The other guard awoke, rubbed his eyes, leapt to his feet when he saw his compatriot, and headed for the beach.

"Coward," Jakov yelled before turning to Kon. "Well, that was easy."

He strode towards his men. Kon bit back tears as he watched Jakov embrace each in turn. They wept openly at his reassurances they were safe. Kon didn't speak their language but it was clear many of them couldn't believe their count was alive.

It took half an hour of frustrating hammering on the chains with the no-too-sharp adze before the captives were at least separated from each other.

"Now we walk back to Termoli," Jakov declared, then he explained the plan to his smiling men.

The smiles left their faces when Drosik strolled into the clearing with half a dozen men. They disappeared into the bushes in the blink of an eye. Kon didn't blame them and was confident he and Jakov and the crew from the *Nunziata* would make short work of the pirate once they arrived.

His blood ran cold when the *Ragusa* sailed slowly into view behind the newcomers. Zara was bound tight to the mainmast, a bloody rag tied around her beloved forehead.

A HIGH PRICE

Zara strained in vain at the thick ropes binding her to the mast. The throbbing pain in the back of her head had lessened, but the ache of dread in her heart threatened to render her witless. Her foolhardy over-confidence had led to this and put their lives in jeopardy.

It had been some time since Drosik had taunted her and she wondered where he had gone. When she heard the unmistakable sound of the anchor being dropped, she narrowed her eyes, trying to make out what was happening on shore as the *Ragusa* hove to. She blinked away the beads of sweat blurring her vision and licked her parched lips.

Kon was there. She sensed his presence. And Jakov with him. Her belly lurched when she made out the hated red shirt. Drosik must have left the ship before it dropped anchor. "Don't trust him," she cried hoarsely, though it was unlikely her warning would be heard over the wind.

A nearby crewman leaned in close and

grinned a toothless grin. The stench of his foul breath sent bile rising in her throat. "Don't worry," he crowed. "You'll soon be free. Your Wolf will agree to Drosik's terms."

A whirlwind raged in her head.

Terms?

Never.

Lupomari's arrival in the *Nunziata* must be imminent. There would be no need to treat with the despicable pirate. And what would Drosik expect in return for her release anyway?

Fear blossomed in the pit of her stomach.

My Wolf? If Drosik was aware of their feelings for one another he would use it against...

No!

"Don't agree to anything," she urged again.

~ ~ ~

When Kon saw Zara was a prisoner on Drosik's ship he inhaled deeply to calm his rage. It didn't work. Seething, he urged Jakov to flee. "Take care of your men. It's vital they remain free. They need you."

Jakov balked. "But my debt to you..."

"Go," he replied, distracted by the wound Zara had evidently suffered. "Your debt is paid once your men are back in Croatia with their families."

The rustle of leaves behind him indicated

Jakov had joined his men in the forest.

"What are your terms, pirate?" he shouted.

Drosik sneered. "No terms, priest. *Signorina* Polani will fetch a king's ransom in the slave market. Such a tasty morsel."

Kon clenched his jaw and eyed the *scimitar* lying on the rock where they'd smashed apart the chains. One blow would be sufficient to lop off the pirate's head, but he was one man against several. "Why not flee south?"

"It appears you've deprived me of the slaves —my most lucrative prize. I want you to be aware of the price you've paid for your pious foolishness."

Kon racked his brain for a plan to get Zara off the *Ragusa*. "I will pursue you to the ends of the earth if you harm a hair on her head."

Drosik scoffed. "You'd have to be alive and I don't intend to permit that."

Kon was conflicted. If he succeeded in killing the pirate there was no guarantee he hadn't given instructions to his crew to sail on anyway. Where in the name of all the saints was Lupomari with the *Nunziata*?

He tried one last ploy. "You may kill me, but Zara's uncle is the Doge of Venezia. He will seek vengeance for such an offence against his family. There won't be a port anywhere in the Adriatic or the Mediterranean where you'll be safe."

The sly grin disappeared.

Kon knew what he had to do. "Let her go and take me instead."

~ ~ ~

"See," the foul-mouthed sailor goaded as he untied the ropes binding Zara.

She spat in his face. He scowled and brandished a fist at her, but she didn't flinch. Muttering, he averted his sullen gaze and removed the last of the ropes.

She looked around the ship, seeking a way to escape, but Drosik's men seemed to be everywhere.

The moron shoved her to the side. "Over you go."

She braced her legs. "You expect me to jump into the sea?"

He took a step towards her. "Or I throw you in."

She took a last look at the shore. Kon had picked up one of the eastern swords and seemed to be holding Drosik and his men at bay. Why was the pirate letting her go?

Seeing no alternative and sickened by the prospect of the lout's filthy hands on her body, she climbed up onto the wale and dove into the clear water, confident the beach wasn't far away. She was prepared this time for the shock of the impact, but memories of tumbling into the water with the boy assailed her. If only she'd held onto him.

She resurfaced quickly, coughing out seawater as she tried to get her bearings. The pain in her head hammered when she espied Kon being goaded into a small rowboat at the point of the *scimitar* in Drosik's grip.

"No," she yelled, choking on salty water.

She struck out for the shore, her progress hampered by the leaden dread in her limbs. It was a nightmare. She was swimming but making no headway.

Exhausted, she crawled up the beach and looked back at the *Ragusa*. Sailors were hauling the rowboat over the side and Kon was nowhere to be seen.

She retched into the sand, shaking with grief and anger when the ship weighed anchor and she espied Drosik on the forecastle, jauntily waving his green hat.

DESPAIR

After being forced at the point of his *scimitar* to board the *Ragusa*, Kon glanced back at the shore, relieved to see Zara had made it to the beach. She was alone, but he wagered Jakov would return, and at least she was out of Drosik's clutches.

He turned to congratulate the pirate on for once keeping his word when a blow to the back of the head rendered him witless.

He wasn't sure how much time had passed when he regained his wits, but the ship was under sail and an ache throbbed in his temples. He tried to press his hands to his head, but discovered his wrists and ankles were tightly bound. Mercifully, he'd been tied with rope and not chained.

He seemed to be lying in a pool of water in some kind of confined space. His gut knotted when he realized he'd been shoved beneath a rowing thwart. He tried to wriggle out but there was no room to maneuver and he was wedged in tight.

A booted foot appeared. By the sound of the tapping above his head he assumed the other foot was atop the bench. He wasn't surprised to hear Drosik's taunting voice. "I see you've awakened."

"There's no need for this," he replied. "I surrendered to you voluntarily."

"Ah, but now you are my captive and I cannot risk losing my profit."

An alarm sounded in the back of Kon's aching head. "Profit?"

"The Fatimids will pay well for a strapping young man they can in turn sell to the Mamluk army."

An icy prickle marched up Kon's spine. "The Pope has forbidden the sale of Christians to Islamists."

Drosik chuckled. "True, but the Fatimids have been known to cut out the tongues of prisoners who protest they are followers of the hated Christian God. You're swarthy enough to pass for a Mohammedan."

The irony struck Kon. If he proclaimed his rediscovered faith, he risked losing his tongue. He had bitter experience of the brutality of the Fatimid traders. "The *Nunziata* will catch you before you can reach Bari."

Drosik braced both feet on the wet planking. "The *Nunziata* won't be going anywhere for a while. Do you think I am such a fool not to recognize her in the lagoon?"

His captor's laughter faded as he walked away. Kon feared he might retch, unthinkable in the tight space. The uncertainty as to the *Nunziata's* fate gnawed at him. The notion of being sold as a slave in the selfsame market where his troubles had begun churned his gut. A life of servitude fighting in an army of slaves loomed. His one consolation was that Zara had been spared the degradation, but the prospect of never seeing her again filled him with despair.

~ ~ ~

Zara sat on the beach and watched the *Ragusa* disappear. "Wolf," she whispered to the wind, bereft at the loss of the only man she'd ever loved. Dread turned her blood to ice when she contemplated the fate awaiting him if Drosik succeeded in reaching Bari.

Something untoward had happened to her beloved ship. It was the only explanation for its failure to come to the rescue.

She barely had the strength to turn when a rustling noise in the trees indicated she was no longer alone. It was a relief to see Jakov and his bedraggled men emerge from the bushes.

He hunkered down beside her and peered out to sea. "We'll save him," he reassured her.

"Why didn't you fight to help him?" she wailed, ashamed that her presence aboard the *Ragusa* had obviously been the reason. Neither man would have risked jeopardising her life.

He took her hands and helped her to her feet. "Something must have happened to your ship," he said. "We assumed she would be here by now."

She nodded woodenly, thankful he hadn't asked how she came to be aboard the pirate ship. How to explain the stupidity of William's soldiers and her own cocksure foolhardiness?

"At least your men are free," she murmured lamely, guilt-ridden that she'd been the one who'd contracted to transport them in the first place. She glanced at their faces, aware Polani ships had carried many such honest men, women and children to harsh servitude in foreign climes. Kon had opened her eyes to the evil of it. "I'm sorry," she murmured.

He remained stern-faced. "We must begin the walk back to Termoli."

The prospect of walking for hours in the hot sun made her want to retch again, but it was the only way to find out what had happened to the *Nunziata* and hopefully begin the pursuit.

"We'll walk upriver first," Jakov explained. "You can quench your thirst and bathe your head wound. It's a long trek."

She touched a hand to the rag covering the gash on her scalp she'd forgotten. "What will you do when we get there?"

"Whatever is necessary to save Konrad von Wolfenberg."

His promise was a tiny island of hope in a sea of despair.

~ ~ ~

Kon baked in his prison for the rest of the afternoon. No one came near him. He was offered neither food nor water. Thirst raged. It was a blessed relief when the sun went down and the air cooled, but the ship sailed on through the night and soon his teeth were chattering.

He must have eventually surrendered to exhaustion, his sleep troubled by visions of his father weeping. He was rudely awakened when cold water was thrown over him. He licked his lips, hoping to glean a drop of moisture, only to discover it was seawater he'd been doused with.

"You stink, slave," the sailor who'd chucked the water exclaimed.

He narrowed his eyes against the first grey streaks of dawn, bursting to ask what the fool expected of a man shut up in a box, but he deemed it better to save his strength.

The *Ragusa* sailed on for hours, propelled by a strong wind. Hunger gnawed. Even a weevil-infested biscuit would taste good. It was apparent his situation was desperate. He'd greatly underestimated Drosik, but dwelling on regrets and recriminations would only add to his torment. He decided to concentrate on the two things that might keep a flicker of hope alive; his faith and his beloved Zara. He lapsed into a stupor until he was dragged back to reality by the insistent call of oystercatchers and the stink of fish guts. They had reached Bari.

DREAD

Zara feared her trembling legs might not sustain her any further after four hours of trying to keep pace with Jakov. She'd lived a life of comfortable ease and wasn't prepared for strenuous exercise. When the tower of Termoli castle came in sight at last she was tempted to fall to her knees in thanksgiving the ordeal was over.

Then she sobered. Kon was likely suffering far worse torments than she, and they had yet to begin the pursuit. She surmised Drosik would head for Bari. The Pope had forbidden the sale of Christians to Mohammedans, but Jakov and his men were living proof such rules meant nothing to slavers.

The tide was out when they reached the lagoon. She was torn between laughing and crying when she espied the *Nunziata* mired in the mud. She'd feared her beloved ship lay at the bottom of the sea.

Lupomari was pacing on the dock and hurried towards them. "Madonna," he exclaimed, bracing her as she staggered into his arms. "I beg your forgiveness, *Signorina* Polani. We were unable to give chase. The cursed pirate damaged our rudder. We had to wait for low tide for Rospo to make repairs. Thanks be to the saints you are safe."

She struggled to stand on her own feet, anger endowing her with new strength. "But Konrad Wolf is not. Drosik has taken him prisoner. We must get underway as soon as possible."

She lay flat on the dock and peered down to the brown mud under the flat-bottomed hull where Rospo and others labored to repair the rudder. She heard hammering and cursing but couldn't see them. "How goes it?" she shouted, holding her nose against the reek of the sea's detritus.

The noise ceased.

"Smashed," Rospo called back.

"Can it be repaired?"

There was a long pause.

"*Sì.*"

She breathed again. "How long?"

"Hour."

The hammering resumed. She scrambled to her feet and turned to Jakov. "I cannot ask you to come with us. You must see to the safety of your men."

The Croat smiled. "Konrad said the same

thing, but I owe you both a debt and we must aid you. Besides, I've taken a fancy to a certain cog owned by a cruel pirate. She would serve nicely to get me and my men back to Istria. I've stolen many things, what's one more? I will pray for forgiveness."

She marveled he still had his sense of humor after his suffering. "I am grateful. You'll make a fine captain for the *Ragusa*."

Rospo's raspy voice emerged from below. "Two hours."

Jakov must have sensed her frustration at the further delay. "Enough time for us to find sustenance and clothing for my men," he interjected. "And to ponder a new name for our ship."

"I can provide food and clothing," Lupomari said. "Come with me."

A certain William of Loritello should be told of the catastrophe his men had unwittingly provoked. The least he owed her was a good meal and a bath. "Let your men go with my captain, Count Jakov. I suggest you and I pay a visit to the castle."

The freed captives looked hesitantly to their leader, but he reassured them with a nod, then proffered his arm to Zara. "It will be my pleasure," he replied.

~~~

Kon couldn't see anything of the port of Bari from his prison, but the sounds and smells were sickeningly familiar. The gentle rocking of the *Ragusa* at anchor did nothing to calm the dread raging within him.

The cries of gulls reminded him of his incredulity at the first glimpse of slaves being herded off ships years ago.

The clink of chains brought back memories of his horror at watching men and women being treated like dogs.

He recalled the bile that rose up his throat every time he visited the docks and smelled rotting fish.

When he heard foreign voices haggling in the market he relived the blows rained on him by the outraged Fatimids.

Duke Heinrich's angry face loomed. From his twisted mouth emerged the taunt. "Soon it will be your turn."

He had long held the conviction that forced servitude was ungodly. Now as fear and helplessness threatened to stop his heart, he knew why.

He prayed like he'd never prayed before. He begged forgiveness for his disbelief, and pleaded for an acceptance of his fate. He thanked his Savior for the priceless gift of sacrificing his freedom for the woman he loved.

He kept his eyes closed when Drosik came. "I'm off to scout out buyers, priest. My men will get you ready for their inspection."

Rough hands hauled him out of the stinking box. They cut the rope binding his ankles but his legs buckled beneath him. They held him up, tore off his shirt and doused him with seawater again.

Then, an unexpected blessing. A tumbler was thrust into his bound hands. "Drink," a voice admonished.

Trembling, he raised the tumbler to his parched lips and guzzled the watered ale so fast he nigh on choked. He held out the tumbler for more but it was yanked out of his hands.

He heard Drosik's voice speaking Arabic. It was only then he summoned the courage to open his eyes and look into the greedy gaze of the Fatimid who had come to buy him.

He was tempted to laugh at the sight of Drosik's green hat, but the pirate was making a big show of cleaning his filthy nails with the point of a dagger. The message was clear. If he wanted to keep his tongue he'd best remain silent.

He didn't understand the words the two men exchanged but suspected Drosik was describing him as a Mohammedan. If he protested, the fat Arab wouldn't understood German. He was turbaned but wore no face wrap. He wrinkled his bulbous nose in disgust as he perused and poked biceps, belly and thighs.

Kon had an urge to spit in his face, but doubted he could summon enough saliva. He clenched his jaw and conjured memories of swimming in the cool waters of the Elbe as a boy. He'd been brought up to honor his body and the degradation of filth was humiliating.

"Don't worry," Drosik hissed between gritted teeth. "He's using the excuse to lower the price. He knows once you're cleaned up you'll be worth a king's ransom."

A tremor of hatred and fear seized him as the two men wandered off, still haggling.

THE NEW ZARA

William spluttered his disbelief and apparent anger when he learned what had happened as a consequence of his soldiers' actions, and promised they would be reprimanded.

He arranged for a bath to be brought to a chamber for Zara, and invited Jakov to use the facilities in the barracks. "King Ruggero has soldiers stationed here now," he explained sheepishly. "To keep an eye on me. He also takes a dim view of pirates."

She knew a twinge of pity for him, but at least he still lived in his family's castle. "We thank you," she replied, though she worried for Jakov if any soldier espied the manacle around his wrist.

The bath water was tepid, but renewed her spirit. She washed her hair and carefully bathed the wound on her scalp, pleased to feel a scar had begun to form. She hoped there would be no lasting mark.

There was scant chance comfortable clothing would be located. She was reconciled to donning the same outfit after drying her body. There seemed to be a dearth of servants around the place, but she preferred to take care of herself in the circumstances.

She narrowed her eyes at the ragtag Zara Polani who stared back from the silvered glass. Certainly, she was no longer the unconventionally but well-dressed Venetian businesswoman. However, something else had changed. The new Zara was a woman in love who'd known the intimate touch of a passionate man. A determination to rescue her lover from a terrible fate burned in her eyes. She squared her shoulders and signed the cross of her Savior.

Yet, as she made the familiar gesture, she pushed aside doubts about a God who would consign a man like Kon to hell.

When she arrived back in the hall, she discovered Jakov already seated at a table laden with roast chicken, ham and bread. It was meager fare compared to that customarily offered to visitors to the Polani household, but her belly growled.

William nervously invited her to sit.

"He's worried how the king will react if he learns of these matters," she whispered to Jakov as she took her place at table. "Ruggero has striven to maintain good relations with Venezia and my uncle, the Doge."

He nodded in agreement.

Their host made tsking sounds, shaking his head as he sat. "Fine men, those young Saxons. Sons of a count. When the imperial army withdrew, one of them...er, Francesca..."

Zara recognised the wistful look in his eyes. "Lute."

"Yes, yes. Do you know what happened to her? King Ruggero has often berated me for allowing his niece to leave. As if anyone was able to dissuade the hot-headed Sicilian woman from..."

"According to Kon, they married," she interrupted when he faltered.

To her surprise, he looked relieved. Perhaps he wasn't as resigned to Ruggero's dominance as he seemed.

"Good. She is happy and out of her uncle's clutches. You say this pirate has transported young Wolfenberg to Bari?"

Jakov nodded. "It's more than likely."

"Naught I can do then. The king has failed to recapture the town."

She privately doubted William intended to take action. He seemed too lethargic. However, she answered in a conciliatory manner. "A message sent by land would take too long. We will begin pursuit as soon as the *Nunziata* is repaired."

Her words turned out to be prophetic. A footman entered, coughed politely and announced the arrival of one of her crew. "A man of few words," the servant explained, "but I understand the repairs to your ship are complete."

They bade William a hasty farewell and, as expected, found Rospo waiting at the foot of the steps into the castle.

"Is the *Nunziata* fit to sail?" she enquired as they walked briskly to the port.

"She is."

"Has the tide come in?"

"It has."

The corners of Jakov's mouth curled in amusement. "Have my men been fed and clothed?"

Rospo didn't miss a stride. "They have."

"It will be a full crew," Zara remarked.

"It will."

"My men are not sailors," Jakov explained. "But they are willing and able, especially if they believe this voyage might result in the capture of the *Ragusa*."

"Rospo will watch over them," she assured him.

"*Sì*," the steersman confirmed with a rare smile.

Lupomari waved them aboard when they arrived on the dock. Zara was elated to see the pitch had been mostly cleaned off the ship's name. "No gold leaf to be had in Termoli," her captain lamented.

"Once we get home," she reassured him.

As she gained the forecastle it occurred to her that the notion of *home* offered a ray of hope. Mayhap it was a good omen. They would make it back to Venezia alive. She gripped the railing, determined to hold on to her optimism as they weighed anchor and rowed out of Termoli's port.

TOO LATE

Wedged tight in his box, Kon had longed to be upright and free, but now, tied to the mast by his wrists with no opportunity to sit, he feared his legs might buckle.

The sun scorched his bare shoulders and back. The nagging uncertainty churned his innards. He was almost relieved to hear Drosik's nasally voice when the pirate captain returned to the ship. The reek of spirits only aggravated his anguish.

"We've struck a bargain," Drosik crowed as the rope binding Kon to the mast was cut.

He turned on unsteady legs to face his tormentors. Drosik swayed drunkenly, the hat askew on his head. The Arab was alarmingly sober, but a smile tugging at one corner of his thick lips indicated his satisfaction with the transaction.

Drosik clamped a hand on Kon's sunburned shoulder. "I've done you a favor, *priest.*"

His eyes widened as he pressed his hand to his mouth and swallowed a hiccup. "We must hope our fat friend here doesn't understand the word," he jested. "Nigh on ruined the deal."

Kon raised his eyes to heaven and prayed for forbearance.

"Anyway," Drosik drawled. "Be glad. You won't be put on sale in the market. Nizar here is an envoy for the Caliph. We've agreed on a price. You'll be taken straight into the army in Egypt."

Nizar said something in Arabic and held up both hands, fingers spread wide.

"Yes," Drosik explained. "We've set the term at ten years. Then you'll be free. More than generous, don't you think? Nizar wanted twenty."

Kon's hands were still tied, but it wouldn't take much effort to loop his arms around the pirate's scrawny neck and snap it. He might be doing the Arab a favor if he killed Drosik. However, Nizar was armed with a lethal looking curved dagger sheathed at his corpulent middle, and Kon couldn't win against both men.

However, he wasn't a killer, though it seemed he'd be spending the next ten years fighting in one battle or another. Who were the Fatimids at war with anyway?

Ten years.

He choked back regret. Zara would find

someone worthier and marry according to her station. Her belly would never swell with Kon's child, but she'd be free. He'd failed to rescue the girl, but he'd saved the woman he loved.

Nizar pointed to a nearby cog.

"His ship," Drosik explained. "He'll take you aboard shortly. *Bon voyage.*"

Chuckling, he sauntered away and stumbled down the gangplank. No doubt off to spend his profit on more debauchery.

Nizar's friendly expression turned sour. He unsheathed his dagger and sliced through the bindings. Kon rubbed his rope-burned wrists, but his relief was short lived. Nizar beckoned to two Arabs on the dock. As they came aboard, Kon's blood turned to ice when he espied the iron collar and manacles the men carried.

~ ~ ~

Lupomari pushed the *Nunziata* and her crew hard, but there were no complaints. Indeed, a rousing cheer went up when Bari came in sight.

They rowed into the port just before dusk. Zara scanned the forest of masts, her hopes rekindled when she picked out the *Ragusa*.

At a signal from the captain, oars were raised. Everyone aboard the *Nunziata* kept silent while they floated past the pirate ship.

"Looks deserted," Jakov remarked after they docked a short distance away.

Conflicting emotions swirled in Zara's heart. "The absence of guards doesn't bode well for Kon."

"Nor for the rest of our cargo," Lupomari added.

Zara clenched her jaw. "Salt and fabric are of no importance."

Lupomari looked sheepish.

"Your captain understands what's at stake here," Jakov said softly.

Regret for her outburst filled her heart. "I know, and I am sorry, faithful friend."

Without a word, Rospo and Lorenzo hurried off the ship as soon as the gangplank was in place and quickly disappeared into the town.

"They'll find out what's going on," Zara said.

Jakov's eyes widened as he cocked his head to one side. "In the meantime, the *Ragusa* sits, apparently unguarded. Like a juicy plum ripe for the picking."

Zara had been brought up to abhor piracy, but Drosik was a thief with no regard for others. His ship could be put to good use to get Jakov's men home. "I'll turn a blind eye."

However, the small chance Kon might still be aboard forced her to watch as the Istrian and his soldiers stole silently towards the *Ragusa*. They swarmed over the side, apparently encountering no opposition. She peered into the gathering darkness, looking for a sign, hoping against hope to see Kon emerge from the cog.

The signal came, easing her fears. Someone waved a lantern back and forth, male voices were raised in obvious jubilation—Jakov's language—but there was no sign of the man she loved.

They were one step closer to assuring the return home of the slaves who'd been aboard her ship and it was of some consolation that Kon would be elated. But it was a victory bought at a terrible price.

She looked across at the market, empty and silent now, and closed her eyes to ward off the image she conjured of Kon, his beautiful body put on display for greedy slavers. He'd already endured much because of the cursed place.

Jakov returned to the *Nunziata*. "He's not aboard."

She swallowed her disappointment. "No sign of Drosik?"

He shook his head. "Deserted. And your cargo is gone. The pirate is probably celebrating his ill gotten gains."

She startled when Rospo appeared out of the darkness. It was uncanny. The ungainly man moved without the slightest sound. She hadn't seen him on the dock and here he was on the gangplank.

"Dead," he croaked.

A scream lodged in her dry throat. Surely she would have sensed if Kon had died.

"Drosik," Lorenzo explained as he too came aboard. "Throat slit. Folk say he got into an argument with an Arab."

She gripped the railing, swaying with relief, but still consumed with worry. "What of Konrad Wolf?"

"Sold," Rospo replied.

Tears pricked as she looked again at the darkened market.

Lorenzo must have sensed her desolation. "Drosik sold him directly to a Fatimid seeking slaves for the Caliph's army. Some say the one who murdered him."

"But where is he now?" she wailed in a high-pitched voice she barely recognized.

"Feloz."

Her endurance at an end, she glared at her steersman. "Can you not give more than one word responses?"

Rospo averted his gaze, and she instantly regretted her harsh outburst. It was the second time in an hour she'd lost control of her emotions. "I'm sorry," she admitted. "You are as concerned as I am."

Rospo inhaled deeply. "Sailed earlier in the day."

It was the longest string of words she'd heard him utter in five years and she recognized the effort it had taken, but still didn't fully understand.

Lorenzo coughed nervously. "The *Feloz* is the one of the Caliph's ships. She has sailed."

The world seemed to tilt, the dozens of masts became a forest of dark creatures closing in. They were too late. "Was Kon aboard?"

"Chained."

The word was enough to deepen her despair. She couldn't speak, couldn't voice her fear. Conditions for the slaves on her vessel had admittedly not been ideal. On board a Fatimid slaver...

Jakov clenched his jaw. "Headed for *Egipat*, I'll warrant."

"*Egitto*," Rospo confirmed with a vigorous nod.

Her heart broke in two. It was a voyage of nigh on a thousand miles from Bari to Egypt. "A sennight," she murmured.

"With favorable winds," Lupomari agreed. "A fortnight otherwise."

It was impossible. The slaver had a head start. Yet she had to do everything in her power to rescue Kon. It was her fault he had entered hell. "The *Nunziata* will set out in pursuit on the morrow," she declared.

"And the *Pravda*," Jakov said, pointing his thumb toward the *Ragusa*.

She frowned.

"It means *justice* in my language," he explained.

Rospo's enormous eyes shone in the darkness. "*Perfetto*," he exclaimed.

MENAS

A heavy chain connected a ring on the front of Kon's iron collar to that of the man who rowed next to him. The manacles around their wrists were chained to the oar they plied.

Yet Kon considered he was lucky Nizar had selected him as one of twenty rowers. It seemed the fat Arab was the slave-master, not the captain. A *scimitar* bounced on his hip. It looked remarkably like the one he'd surrendered to Drosik, and he suspected something dire had befallen the pirate. Nizar's other weapon was a vicious looking whip, whose knotted thongs he caressed constantly with one beefy hand.

The remaining one hundred or more slaves being transported aboard the *Feloz* languished in every nook and cranny of the hull in a piteous pile of moaning humanity.

He and the other rowers were given a loincloth which provided some relief from the rough wood of the bench. The other captives, including the women, were naked.

The slaves in the hull were chained to each other with manacles and shackles, rendering movement impossible. The Fatimids picked their way through them regularly, stopping to menace and kick at random.

Kon was given water from time to time. It tasted brackish, but the wretches in the pile received nothing.

Many of the captives suffered terribly from seasickness as the ship pitched and rolled in heavy seas. Kon thanked God he was a good sailor and blessed whatever ancestor he'd inherited the trait from. The bodies of those who succumbed to the rigors of the voyage were thrown overboard—after their hands and feet were hacked off, saving their jailers the trouble of unfettering them. Memories of Zara's courage in trying to save Jakov's son from drowning threatened to swamp him.

The winds weren't favorable and strenuous rowing was often necessary to make any progress. Those who in Nizar's judgement didn't pull hard enough flinched under the sting of his whip.

Disgust and hatred churned in Kon's belly. Each time the bile rose in his throat and he feared he could no longer bear the horror, he closed his eyes and tasted again the salty sweetness of Zara's juices. Impulsive and seemingly reckless intimacy became his lifeline.

His oar-mate was the first black man he'd seen since the fateful day of his beating in the Bari market. Initially, as they pulled on the oar he was fascinated by the stark contrast in the color of their skin, but it quickly became apparent black skin chafed by manacles and stung by a whip bled as readily as white skin.

An oarsman, another black man, who had the temerity to speak to his neighbor while rowing was castigated by having his tongue cut out before being tossed into the stinking mass. Drosik hadn't exaggerated the butchery men were capable of.

When the wind blessedly turned in their favor and filled the sail, Nizar smiled at them benevolently and commanded they cease rowing. He stalked off, whip in hand, to attend to something going on amidships he evidently didn't like.

Kon leaned forward to rest his forearms on the oar and whispered his name. "Konrad."

Obliged to lean forward too, the black man glanced warily at Nizar then turned his head to look at Kon. "Menas."

"Saxony," Kon said hoarsely, regretting he'd mentioned his beloved homeland as nostalgia threatened to choke him.

Menas nodded thoughtfully. "Makuria."

Kon had no notion where Makuria was, but the pride and longing in Menas's voice was unmistakable.

He took a guess. "Africa?"

Menas shrugged. "Nubia."

Kon's father had talked of Nubia, an important trading nation, powerful for hundreds of years, but he couldn't recall where it was. Zara would be aware of its exact location.

"On the River Nile," Menas told him.

But he'd spoken in a language Kon understood!

"You speak Greek," Kon retorted with a smile.

Menas returned the smile, his teeth startlingly white in his black face. "And you understand it."

He didn't explain how it was he spoke Greek. Menas was probably a Mohammedan who might use the knowledge of Kon's former religious vocation to his advantage.

"Nubia encompasses the land between the First and Sixth Cataracts," Menas said hoarsely.

Kon frowned, uncertain as to his meaning.

"Of the Nile," Menas explained.

Kon was puzzled. "How is it you speak Greek?"

"Byzantines. Greek used to be our first

language. I speak Coptic too, and my native Dongolawi, of course."

Kon considered it a divine blessing he'd been shackled to a man who was obviously educated. In the years ahead intelligent conversation might save his sanity. Then a thought intruded. "Coptic?"

Menas kept his eyes on Nizar. "Christians and Mohammedans have lived together in peace in my country for centuries. Nubian Christians are loyal to the Coptic Patriarch of Alexandria. Ironic, isn't it, that's where our destiny awaits."

The fickle wind changed again, necessitating a resumption of rowing. Kon heaved on the oar with muscles already spent. He'd have to wait patiently to learn more about his intriguing fellow captive.

NAVIGATING ROUGH WATERS

"We will seek shelter with the Venetian community at the Chiesa di San Marco dei Venezia," Zara explained to Jakov. "They will welcome you even though you aren't Venetian."

"There is a community of Venetians here in Bari?" he asked.

She nodded as the crews made their way through the narrow streets to the *chiesa*. "It has grown steadily since the *church* was built over a hundred years ago by Doge Pietro Orseolo to celebrate the liberation of Bari from the Saracens. It's a safe haven for travellers from my republic. Most of them come and go, traders like my father. The Polani name is well known here."

He grimaced. "We must hope the men who kidnapped me are not among them."

They were welcomed, fed and sheltered. Prayers were offered for the success of their voyage. Zara had to reluctantly agree with suggestions from several of the Venetians that the *Pravda* was the more suitable of the two ships to go in pursuit. She'd be faster and more manoeuvrable in the heavy weather they predicted. A skeleton crew of loyal men was left to guard the *Nunziata* with instructions to sail back to Venezia if they didn't return in a month. The community of San Marco undertook to organise a rotating watch.

Nevertheless, it was difficult to abandon her beloved ship as they set sail on the noon tide the following day. Standing on the forecastle of the *Pravda* with Lupomari and Jakov, she swallowed tears. "We'll see her again," she reassured her captain, aware of the distress he must be feeling.

His jaw remained firmly clenched. "I've been in command of her for nigh on fifteen years and I don't intend for anyone else to be master."

"Well," Jakov interjected, "you can be in charge of the *Pravda* on this voyage. I am no captain, but I need to learn, as do my men."

Zara smiled. "You'll be learning from the best."

Lupomari smiled modestly. "This will be a new endeavor for me as well."

Zara admired her captain. He hadn't hesitated to join the adventure. His life as master of a Polani ship wasn't free of danger but this voyage held unknown risks.

"I surmise they'll head for Alexandria," Lupomari said, "by way of the Ionian Sea. If they sail non-stop, it will be difficult to catch up. Depends on their captain's knowledge of landmarks and the stars." He reached into his leather tunic and pulled out a well-worn little book. He opened it to reveal neat handwritten notes. "I've sailed to Alexandria many times, hence I have my pilot-book of sailing directions. However, he might have compiled a similar record."

Jakov took a keen interest in the scribblings, asking many questions. Zara was as versed in the art of daytime and nocturnal navigation as Lupomari, thanks to her father, but she was happy to let her captain share his expertise, glad to center her thoughts on Kon. If she prayed hard enough, perhaps the Blessed Virgin would carry her entreaties to the Almighty.

She held on to the railing with both hands when the *Pravda* encountered heavy seas and unfavorable winds outside the break-wall. In normal circumstances they might have turned back and waited for better weather.

But time wasn't on their side.

~ ~ ~

As darkness descended a loud argument erupted on the forecastle of the *Feloz*.

"Nizar wants to carry on," Menas gasped

between strokes as he and Kon pulled together, "but the captain is refusing."

Kon didn't have the strength to comment on his comrade's knowledge of yet another language, but prayed the captain got his way.

After long minutes, Nizar stomped into view. It was too dark to see his face but his voice betrayed his anger when he gave the order to raise the oars. He hurried off, brandishing his whip.

The all-too-familiar sound of leather biting into human flesh, followed by shrieks of pain indicated he was taking out his wrath on the unfortunates.

Kon and Menas had by now perfected the art of slumping forward on the oar in unison. Kon was too exhausted to feel disgust. He seemed unable to control his body's persistent trembling. He had to harden his heart and think only of himself if he was to survive.

The ship drifted and he wondered vaguely why the captain hadn't dropped anchor. Then suddenly they were out of the wind and the ship lurched when the anchor touched bottom.

"Tricase on the tip of Italy, I'll wager," Menas said under his breath. "The captain doesn't want to venture into the Ionian Sea in the dark. They say there are depths out there no lead-line has ever fathomed. He must be new at this."

"With any luck he'll drive the ship aground and we'll drown."

"Don't despair, Konrad. I am named for Saint Menas, the patron saint of miracles and wondrous events. We cannot lose hope."

Kon closed his eyes and listened to the gentle lapping of waves against the side of the ship. It reminded him of the night he'd spent watching over Zara. The memory muddled his thinking. "You are a Christian? I've never heard of your blessed saint and I studied religion."

Menas didn't seem to take offence at the doubt in his voice. "Which is the reason you speak Greek. I will tell you of my saint another time. I believe we are actually going to be given sustenance."

Kon opened his eyes. Fatimids were indeed distributing small pottery bowls to the rowers. His expectations weren't high, but at least he wouldn't starve to death. Such would likely be the fate of many in the hull. It was difficult to understand why a slaver would pay for a slave and then starve him.

"A man like Nizar gets his satisfaction from inflicting pain and suffering on others," Menas whispered.

Again the Nubian seemed able to read Kon's thoughts. It only increased his curiosity, but he remained silent when a bowl of grey liquid was thrust at him.

He sipped the tasteless gruel, wishing it was also odorless. "What's the smell?"

"Don't ask," Menas replied.

He held his nose and swallowed the lot in two gulps. "I hope the food improves once we get to where we are going."

Menas shrugged.

Kon shivered, chilled by the night air after sweating for hours in the hot sun. He doubted the Fatimids would provide any kind of covering.

He became alarmed when the Nubian wriggled out of his loincloth, but had to admire the man's resourcefulness when he draped it over his shoulders. He unwrapped his own loincloth and did the same.

Menas shuffled closer. "We can either freeze or share our body heat."

In different circumstances Kon might have punched out those white teeth, but the Nubian was right. They edged closer until their bodies touched.

"Will you pray with me, Konrad?"

He nodded, filled with a serene sense of being in a holier place than he'd been in a long while. They prayed in silence, each man sending his petitions heavenward before slumping into an exhausted sleep.

PURSUIT

The *Pravda* sailed on into the night. Lupomari instructed Jakov how to use the stars to navigate and stay on course. "But it's vital to have a good steersman as well," he pointed out. "A man who knows the winds."

"Like Rospo," Jakov replied.

Lupomari nodded. Everyone was aware Rospo's skill had kept them going in the heavy seas and unfavorable winds they'd battled throughout the day.

"By dawn we should reach the tip of Italy," Zara told them, "especially if the favorable winds blowing now continue all night."

Jakov leaned towards her. "You must get some sleep."

She agreed reluctantly and wandered off to the stern-castle. The only thing left of the *Nunziata's* original cargo were the animal skins used to protect the goods from the elements. They'd been brought aboard the *Pravda* and arranged into a sleeping area of sorts. She collapsed onto the pile, and gazed up at the stars. Sleep was elusive, but it wasn't the odor of mildew clinging to the hides that kept her awake. This ship had transported Kon to Bari from Termoli and the certainty of Drosik's cruel treatment lay like a lead ball in her belly.

A worse ache pressed on her temples. Whatever he had endured at Drosik's hands was likely nothing compared to what he was suffering aboard the slave ship. She'd heard horror stories about slavers, but thinking on such tales might lead to madness.

His constant presence in her thoughts and dreams reassured her he still lived.

She came to her knees and made the sign of her Savior. "I confess my wantonness," she murmured, hands clasped in prayer, "but I beseech you not to punish Konrad Wolf for it. The sin is mine alone and it was I caused him to give up his freedom. Guide our ship so that we might deliver him from his torment." She swallowed hard. "It was not my intention to entice him away from his calling. I swear not to tempt him again if only..."

The prospect of a life without the nourishing warmth of Kon's body pressed against her was too much to bear and she curled her knees to her chest on the hides and wept.

A humming drifted to her ears from somewhere above. Raspy...off-key...a lullaby she hadn't heard since childhood.

Rospo was crooning her to sleep.

~ ~ ~

As dawn broke, Nizar bellowed a wake-up call. Surprised he'd slept, Kon peered up at the steep cliff walls that had sheltered them overnight.

Menas covered his mouth with the end of his loincloth as he readjusted it around his hips."The last of Italy."

If his oar-mate was right, they were about to row into the Ionian Sea. Kon had learned enough about winds from Rospo to know the steady gust teasing the sail would mean easier going—provided it continued.

His prayer was granted when the wind filled the leather sail and the ship picked up speed. His aching muscles needed the respite. He considered leaving the loincloth draped across his shoulders as protection from the sun which would soon be hot enough to burn off another layer of his skin. But he felt nervously vulnerable. Nizar was unpredictable.

When he stood awkwardly and braced his knees to wrap the cloth back around his waist and between his legs the cruel tyrant stared at his groin, licking his sneering lips.

Two Fatimids began distributing bowls of the same obnoxious gruel to the rowers, losing their balance several times as the ship made headway.

When their task was complete, Nizar directed them to the now-silent pile of pitiful wretches and they began culling the newly-dead, hacking off limbs and chucking the mutilated bodies over the side.

"Much more of this and I'll go mad," Kon murmured into the grey liquid.

"Keep the faith," Menas muttered back.

His new friend was right. He had to turn to his faith for strength because there was no hope of rescue. It was unlikely Zara would risk the *Nunziata* even if she had discovered where he was being taken. They barely knew each other. She was the woman he'd have married if the fates had been kind, but did she feel the same inexorable alchemy?

If he wanted to avoid a life of brutal servitude, he'd have to start plotting a way to escape. Preoccupied with the impossibility of every scheme he conjured, he fell into a doze. He wasn't sure how much time had passed when raised voices in the stern-castle drifted to his ears. He narrowed his eyes at Menas.

"They are worried. There's another ship, far behind," the black man whispered.

~~~

Lupomari's shout woke Zara from a fitful sleep. She sat up and rubbed her eyes, awed by nature's grandeur as they sailed past the rugged grey cliffs of Tricase.

Jakov hunkered down beside her. "There's a vessel ahead."

"You look exhausted," she replied, nigh on swallowing a yawn when his words penetrated the fog in her brain. She scrambled to her feet. "A ship? Is it the *Feloz*?"

"Too far away to tell, and Lupomari doesn't want to get too close."

Nervous excitement tightened her throat. "I'll take his place on the forecastle so you can both get some sleep. Use the hides. They stink, but they're soft."

She climbed the fist few steps of the sterncastle, relieved to see one of Jakov's men had taken over from Rospo. Her loyal crewman lay curled up on the decking, snoring loudly, his several chins vibrating with each exhaled snort.

She lifted her face to the wind. "We're making good speed. We must hope this fair weather keeps up. The Ionian Sea is no place to encounter a storm."

Jakov lay on his side on the skins. "But favorable winds also help our prey."

She nodded. "It may come down to tactics. Sometime on the morrow we'll pass the Ionian Islands. We Venetians are experts at playing cat-and-mouse at sea."

Jakov frowned. "Why are you doing this?"

She averted her gaze. "It is my fault Kon faces a future as a slave. I owe him a debt."

Jakov smiled. "I understand debts, but there is more, isn't there? You're in love with him."

She sensed it wasn't a question. "Yes, I will go to the ends of the earth to get him back, if I have to."

He chuckled. "I'm confident it won't come to that."

HEAVEN AND HELL

The reign of terror continued aboard the *Feloz* for a second day, and on into the night. It seemed favorable winds had restored the captain's confidence in his navigational skills.

Kon, Menas and the other surviving oarsmen endured intervals of strenuous rowing interspersed by fitful dozes, their only sustenance the insipid gruel and sips of brackish water.

As a youth Kon had boasted to his siblings of his strict adherence to fasting rituals required by the Church. Now the painful reality of near-starvation gnawed his belly. He wouldn't last a year if this regimen carried on, never mind ten.

Nizar's brutality had thinned the ranks of the slaves in the hull. Fewer now remained to stare blankly into their own oblivion, apparently resigned to their fate.

Nightmares stalked Kon's brief periods of sleep. He cheered at bloodying Heinrich's nose with a well-aimed blow, laughed hysterically when he lopped off Nizar's head with one swipe of the *scimitar*, and wept as he watched his mother's coffin being lowered into the ground.

Menas nudged him awake frequently.

Worried his nightmares would incur Nizar's wrath, or worse still drag him into madness, he conjured visions of his brothers and sister, his beloved parents, Zara.

In the end there was only Zara.

"Is she your wife?" Menas whispered sometime on the third day.

He must have uttered his beloved's name. "No."

Menas waited, but further explanation remained lodged in Kon's throat.

"I am acquainted with a woman of the same name. A Venetian."

Kon swallowed his thirst and looked away, his confused mind trying to solve the unlikely coincidence Menas had suggested.

"Or rather I knew her father," the Nubian added. "A trader. Owner of a fleet of ships."

Kon opened his mouth to reply, but a shout from the forecastle caught their attention.

"Land to larbord," Menas translated. "Probably Kerkyra."

The name meant nothing.

"The largest of the Ionian islands."

Kon took advantage of Nizar's preoccupation

with the newly-sighted land. "I might have gone mad by now were it not for your presence," he murmured. "I thank God for your companionship. You've never faltered, though you've suffered as much as any of us."

Menas lay a gentle hand atop his. "My strength lies in having travelled this road before and been delivered from my torment."

Kon thought he might have misheard the faintly whispered words. "This isn't the first time you've been enslaved?"

"I escaped once, only to fall again into the clutches of slavers. There are many in this world who believe every black man belongs in chains. They do not consider they might be kidnapping a prosperous trader respected in his own fertile land and beyond. Zara's father recognized the worth of Nubia and her people. He and I profited from our association. We gained wealth and a strong friendship."

Kon gasped. "You knew it was the same man."

"Yes, I discerned it from your reaction when I told you of my acquaintance with him."

"But how did you gain your freedom?"

"It's a long story, for another time, when Nizar is once more busy with other matters."

Kon was humbled. If he ever escaped this hell and then tumbled into it again, anger would consume him. Menas, however, seemed resigned. Or was it hope kept him going?

~ ~ ~

Zara dragged her salt-stung eyes away from the distant ship she had to hope was the *Feloz* to gaze at the shores of Kerkyra.

"Have you been there?" Jakov asked.

"I came to these islands once, with my father," she replied, recalling halcyon days spent exploring the island.

"I've heard of Kerkyra's scenic beauty from travellers."

"The islands along this coast are breathtaking. Later we'll pass Zante. Polani ships call there sometimes to load tar."

He raised an eyebrow. "Tar?"

"Tar makes a better seal for boats than pitch. The ancient Greeks used to dredge it up from the bottom of a large lake on the island using myrtle branches fastened to the end of long poles. It's not done much differently now, except the ships don't use the tar to seal the hulls here—which is what the ancient Athenians did. These days its collected in pots ready for shipping. My father kept some of it for our vessels and traded the rest. It's a smelly and unpleasant task for the men who have to load the stuff."

Jakov grinned. "Which wasn't your job."

She laughed. "No. There are caves you can only reach by sea. Rospo rowed me and my father to see one of them in a rowboat. When you dip your hand in the water, your skin turns bright blue."

"I've heard of the phenomenon." He held up his hand, evidently trying to conjure an image of it turning blue. "It must be alarming."

"Disconcerting, yes, but when you take your hand out of the water, it's the normal color."

He put his noticeably darker hand next to Zara's on the wooden railing. "Does it have the same effect on all skin colors?"

She shrugged. "I suppose. Rospo's has a green tinge you've probably noticed, but he wouldn't dip his hand. Afraid, I think."

"I doubt he fears anything. Superstitious, mayhap?"

"Well, the caves are eerie. I wouldn't like to be in one alone." She shivered. "Especially with the frequent earthquakes these islands experience. As soon as my father described the destruction they can cause I wanted to leave and never come back. If you were in a cave when a tremor happened the whole cliff might fall in on you. Venezia isn't perfect but at least the earth doesn't move."

He winked. "But one day your fair city might drown beneath the waters of her canals."

It was a common taunt levelled at Venetians by rival states jealous of *La Serenissima's* power and wealth. Zara ignored it with the haughty indifference instilled in those who were proud to call the *Serene Republic* their home.

NO REAL PLAN

For Kon, closing his eyes and escaping into a dream world when they weren't rowing was preferable to watching the slaves in the hull slowly rot in the unforgiving sun.

Zara filled his dreams now. He sifted his fingers through her hair, pecked a kiss on her nose, admired the tilt of her proud chin, brushed his thumbs over rigid nipples and cupped her tempting bottom. He gazed into emerald eyes and sucked on her toes. He slowly peeled off her clothes then stood back to drink in her nakedness. Her smile bade him *welcome aboard*. He nestled his *rute* at her opening and...

"Get ready to row. We're coming into land," Menas muttered under his breath, jolting Kon from his reverie.

The sweat on his body turned to ice. Was it possible they'd already reached Egypt? "Alexandria?"

Menas shook his head. "One of the islands. Maybe Zante. Vessels pull in there to buy pots of tar and take on supplies."

Kon scanned the crowded hull in disbelief. "Where are they going to put pots of tar?"

"Nizar will make room one way or the other. Tar is more valuable than slaves. Men will be expected to load the stuff, and I doubt the Fatimids will do manual labor."

It took a moment for the deeper meaning of Menas's words to penetrate the throbbing ache in Kon's head. "We'll be taken off the ship."

"And maybe unchained from each other."

"But what good is escaping on an island in the middle of the sea?"

Menas winked. "Who mentioned escape? It will simply be a chance to get away from your stink, my friend."

Kon chuckled at the jest. "Right. Never thought I'd look forward to hauling tar."

"Careful you don't get any on your skin or they'll not tell us apart!"

Once again Menas had lifted Kon's spirits with his sense of humor, but more importantly he'd sparked a flicker of hope. "We must keep our eyes open."

"Take care. Nizar will watch us like a hawk watches the field-mouse who thinks he is scurrying around undetected."

It was true the chances of escape were slim, but Kon's heart beat faster when the sail came down.

The ship changed direction.

They took up the oar and pulled until the *Feloz's* flat bottom touched sand.

"Zante," Menas confirmed as the anchor played out.

Kon looked up at the forbidding cliffs towering over the ship. "Who knew tar came from places like this?"

"Given the size of the Polani fleet, I'll warrant Zara is aware of it," Menas whispered.

The mention of her name renewed Kon's hopes. Perhaps an opportunity to be free would come here on Zante.

"Keep the faith, Konrad," Menas reminded him as Nizar lumbered towards them.

~ ~ ~

Zara gaped in disbelief at the empty horizon. "Where are they?" she wailed in exasperation.

"My guess is they've pulled into Zante," Lupomari replied softly.

She inhaled deeply, grateful for her faithful captain's calming presence. "Of course. I should have foreseen that. It's a regular port of call for many of our ships, why not the Caliph's?"

Lupomari agreed. "We'll come about."

A worry nagged. "Be careful they don't see us approach. They've probably been nervous about a ship following them anyway."

He took out his pilot-book. "If they've stopped for tar, they'll be in the bay to the south-west, near Keriou. I'll set a course for the inside passage and bring us in near Laganas. We can anchor out of sight behind a large rock in the bay."

The crew responded efficiently to the new orders to turn the *Pravda*. She noticed Jakov's men seemed comfortable with their tasks.

"Your Croats are proving to be good sailors," she told him. "They've taken well to a life on the sea."

He smiled proudly. "At least they have a life now, and are grateful for it. They will do everything they can to aid in this venture."

She fixed her gaze on the wooded slopes as they passed the distant shore on the larbord side. "I can't see the *Feloz*," she told Jakov, "therefore I assume they can't see us."

"What's the plan?" he asked.

She chewed on her bottom lip. "We pray God will show us the way to free Kon."

"In other words there is no plan."

"No," she admitted reluctantly. "But we must remain hopeful."

TERREMOTO

Relief and an unexpected sense of loss warred within Kon when Nizar removed the chain linking the iron collar around his neck to Menas. His hopes rose when their manacles were loosed from the oar and the last link joining them was unfastened. His spirits faltered when the slave-master ordered leg irons be clamped on their ankles.

Kon had longed to stand upright and walk again, yet when he was prodded out of the rowing bench at the point of a scimitar he couldn't make his legs work. He tottered like a child taking his first shaky steps. He made slow progress along with the twenty oarsmen who shuffled down the gangplank. Directly in front of him, Menas swayed alarmingly. Kon put a hand to his elbow, feeling the caress of Nizar's whip on his shoulder as a reward.

"My thanks," his friend muttered without turning around.

Once on the beach Kon had an urge to fall to his knees in grateful thanks at being on *terra firma* again. He looked back at the sea, filled with a longing to cleanse his body, but Nizar kept them moving. They crossed the beach and followed a well-traveled sandy path shaded by pine trees that led eventually through an olive grove.

Pungent fumes assailed Kon's nostrils well before they emerged from the grove and arrived at a large wooden lean-to crammed with pots of different shapes and sizes, all stacked together haphazardly. Blackened rims confirmed their contents.

The handful of swarthy men who came out to greet Nizar and his henchmen spoke in Greek, but it was evident the Fatimids didn't understand. Loud haggling over price ensued.

In a previous life, he would have enjoyed the relatively short walk from the beach, but in his weakened state he was already close to exhaustion and had a raging thirst. The prospect of carrying one of the pots back to the ship filled him with apprehension.

Nizar's smug smile indicated when a satisfactory bargain had been struck. Two skeletal men appeared from the shadows within the shed. They wore filthy loincloths and were smeared with so much tar it was impossible to ascertain the true color of their skin and hair. Kon assumed they too were slaves from the way they were shoved around by the Greeks.

He might be destined for a life of forced military service but the prospect seemed preferable to the hell these wretches must endure every day of their lives.

The rowers were prodded back into a line. The Greek slaves brought out a pot the size of a toddling child and loaded it onto the back of the first rower, securing it in place by means of a strap around his forehead that was attached to the pot's handles. The man's legs nearly buckled, but a Fatimid pushed him on his way back to the ship. He staggered down the path and out of sight, the Arab on his heels.

When Kon's turn came, the slaves carried out a smaller pot, but Nizar shook his head, pointing to the largest vessel. They retrieved the pot he indicated and Kon had to go down on one knee, gritting his teeth as they struggled to lift it onto his back. When the strap was placed around his forehead he leaned forward, fearing his neck might break. He swallowed his revulsion when tar spilled onto his skin, determined not to give Nizar the satisfaction of seeing fear or weakness. His prayer for the strength to stand was answered when he managed to get to his feet, though pain arrowed through every muscle. He braced his legs, gripped the strap and set off towards the ship, escorted by one of the Fatimids. If he tripped on the leg shackles and fell he had no doubt he was a dead man.

He eventually staggered up the gangplank and was relieved of the heavy pot by two of the other rowers. His aching back suddenly felt chilled without the warmth of the pottery pressed against it. Panting hard, he turned to see Menas shuffling up the gangplank with a burden not much smaller than his own.

"Seems we're the favored ones," the Nubian muttered as Kon helped remove the load from his tar-spattered back.

The new cargo was being stowed under the stern-castle, which meant less space for the slaves, but no murmur of discontent rose from the ones remaining.

Any hope all the tar had been delivered to the ship was dashed when Nizar appeared and gave the order the rowers be herded back to the shed.

~ ~ ~

Zara paced back and forth on the forecastle of the *Pravda*.

"You're making us dizzy," Jakov complained, though she sensed in his own way he was trying to reassure her.

"We should be doing something," she replied, "not simply sitting here hidden behind a rock."

"One option is to sail to the southern tip of Zante and try to see what's going on," Lupomari suggested. "If we knew the size of the *Feloz's* crew we might contemplate boarding her."

Zara shook her head. "We'd loose a lot of good men, and the Fatimids might kill the slaves rather than surrender them."

She'd always been proud of her ability to make difficult decisions, but now her head was stuffed with the wool of a thousand sheep. She sensed Kon's presence nearby, yet was helpless to do anything to help free him. Dread trickled in her veins.

She looked heavenward. "*Dio*, come to our aid," she whispered.

She gradually became aware that seabirds soaring on the breeze had ceased their constant, raucous calls. Only the creak of the *Pravda's* rocking timbers broke the eerie silence. Lupomari and Jakov exchanged frowning glances. Doom hung in the suddenly still air.

Gooseflesh marched across her nape when Rospo bellowed from the stern-castle. "Weigh anchor."

Lupomari echoed the order without hesitation and Zara had no objection. They'd both learned over the years to trust Rospo's instincts.

The oarsmen scrambled to their thwarts.

"Row," Rospo yelled. "Row hard."

As the *Pravda* slowly pulled away from the rock into deeper water, a deafening roar stopped Zara's heart.

She covered her ears and looked back to Zante in the distance. Her mouth fell open. It was as if the cliffs had risen up to shake off the forests covering them.

"*Terremoto*," she breathed, recalling her father's description of the destruction earthquakes had wrought in the Greek islands in the past. Kon was caught up in the terror somewhere amid the uprooted trees, the crumbling rocks, but her immediate concern had to be for the *Pravda*. Rospo's intuition had given them a chance to outrun a tidal wave if one came.

She cupped her hands to her mouth. "Hoist the sail," she shouted. "Head for the open sea."

~ ~ ~

When the shaking began, the Fatimids ran out of the olive grove and back towards the ship, screeching in Arabic.

Kon's heart stopped. Was the world coming to an end?

"Earthquake," Menas shouted above the roar. "Follow me."

Kon reeled like a drunkard, barely avoiding a large crack in the earth that opened up beneath his shackled feet. The Nubian stretched his arms around the trunk of an olive tree. "Join hands," he urged. "We can't hold on separately because of the chains, but together..."

Kon pressed his body to the tree and grasped his comrade's hands. The bark bit into his face, the links of the chain dug into his chest. They clung together for endless minutes, tightening their grip when the roots snapped loose from the trembling ground and the tree tilted alarmingly. Dust rose up from the tormented earth, turning daylight into a choking fog.

Suddenly there was an eerie silence.

After minutes that seemed like an eternity, coughing began in the distance...then cries of pain...muffled shouts of distress.

Discovering he was still hanging from the nearly uprooted tree, Kon blinked the grit out of his eyes, and peered around the trunk. His friend was covered in a layer of dust. "Your skin has turned white," he jested.

"Now that would be a miracle," Menas replied with a tight smile, "but the worst may not be over."

THE SEA'S FURY

"We should see to the slaves on the ship," Kon said, looking around cautiously as he braced his legs and let go of his comrade's hands. "If there's a chance to free them…"

Menas hesitated. "A tidal surge may yet come," he warned.

Kon had no notion of what his friend meant. The tide had come in quickly to swamp the army's tents during the occupation of Termoli years ago, but there'd been little damage. "Nevertheless, we're alive, thanks to your quick thinking."

Without waiting for a reply he hurried along the path, cursing the shackles as he climbed over uprooted trees and strode over deep fissures.

He heard Menas behind him as he came to the beach, astonished at the sight he beheld. Fatimids lay here and there crushed beneath boulders that had fallen from the cliffs. He stared at the bloodied bodies, reliving the heart-stopping terror of the rocks sliding from the surrounding peaks in the Pale Mountains. A lifetime ago.

Menas's hand on his shoulder jolted him from his shock. "Look at the ship."

The flat-bottomed *Feloz* lay on her side, mired in sand, her mast gone, her hull riddled with gaping holes.

He looked back at what had been a sheer cliff when they'd pulled in a scant hour before. "The whole thing came down," he rasped in disbelief. "Just shattered."

Menas pulled his arm. "More importantly, the tide has gone out too quickly. It's an ill omen."

Kon looked out to sea. As far as the eye could see there was nothing but sand. Then, on the distant horizon he saw a speck. "There's a ship out there."

A memory of a dream surfaced. Zara the figurehead. "It's the *Ragusa*."

"It doesn't matter, we must get away from the beach," Menas insisted, clearly agitated.

"There may be survivors," Kon replied, looking for a way to climb aboard.

Menas heaved an exasperated sigh then knelt beside the ruined ship, fingers meshed. Kon accepted the offer and clung to the wood as his friend strained to lift him. He crawled up like a crab, falling over the side onto the decking.

Most of the tar pots lay smashed to pieces,

their contents oozing slowly to cover the entire hull. It had taken the last of his strength and willpower to carry the pot aboard, but satisfaction rippled through him.

But his pleasure fled when he saw the bodies of the slaves. Every one had perished beneath the hail of rocks. Fury filled him when a pitiful moan drew his gaze to Nizar. The monster lay pinned under the fallen mast, arms flailing in the black goo, the stolen *scimitar* waving uselessly in one hand, the whip in the other.

He tasted the acrid desire for vengeance. Not only for himself but for Menas, and for the wretches Nizar had slowly tortured to death. He waded carefully into the tar and yanked the *scimitar* from the Arab's grip. Holding it tightly in both hands, he raised the curved blade above his head.

"*Rahma*," Nizar begged.

The desperation in the man's eyes clearly showed his plea was for *mercy*, but his perverse cruelty had purged every last drop of it from Kon's heart.

He clenched his jaw and made ready to lop off the slave-master's head.

A shout from Menas drew his attention. His comrade had managed to make it up the side and now clung to the top of the wale. "Justice is not yours to dispense, Konrad. God has been

188

merciful to us, but we must get to higher ground."

Kon flexed his biceps and gritted his teeth, but the certainty Menas was right calmed the raging beast within. Nizar already wore the mask of death. Justice had been served.

He straightened his shoulders, threw down the weapon and looked out to sea, hoping to catch another glimpse of the ship he believed Zara had brought to his rescue. He narrowed his eyes, not quite believing the enormous wall of water rushing towards the beach.

~ ~ ~

The swell lifted the *Pravda*. For long moments no one on board breathed as the ship floated in mid air. Then she settled and the swell moved on. Towards Zante.

"You saved us, Rospo," she shouted. "Now follow the wave."

Her steersman smiled briefly, though he seemed troubled. The crew added their loud agreement, but the hubbub quieted as the ship came about and they watched the wave ahead of them grow rapidly into a wall of water taller than any ship. It loomed over Zante like an avenging angel.

"We must hope he isn't on the beach," Jakov said hoarsely.

"Nor on the ship," she murmured.

"The tar pits are a little further inland," Lupomari offered. "If he is there…"

"Drop anchor," Rospo urged.

She echoed his order, mortified that her single-minded determination to aid Kon had again put others in danger. They were close enough to the beach now to make out a vessel directly in the path of the giant wave.

She watched in growing horror as the angry sea smashed into the island, picking up the ship and hurling it against the cliff like a child's plaything.

"No one could survive such a catastrophe," Lupomari said gruffly.

"Kon," she sobbed, knowing all hope was gone.

~ ~ ~

Propelled by sheer terror over the side of the *Feloz*, Kon followed Menas, running back into the trees as fast as the shackles allowed. Sand and grass stuck to the wet tar on the soles of his feet and actually helped him keep his balance in the uneven terrain.

His heart pounded in his ears, louder than the sound of trees and rocks being mowed down by the oncoming surge. Breathless, they rushed into the clearing, astonished to see the rowers who'd survived sitting huddled together in the shed.

"Run," Menas shouted, but it was too late. The wave overtook them. They were lifted off their feet and carried along on a raging river of uprooted trees, branches, planks, plants and animals—some dead, others struggling to keep their heads above water.

Kon was dragged under more than once. He managed to surface after each terrifying dunking, but his endurance was ebbing. He accepted it was only a matter of time before he drowned.

He vaguely heard a shout over the din. Not too far away, Menas had entangled his chains in the branches of a floating tree. Recognizing it as his only hope, he struck out, fighting his way through the debris until his hand grasped a limb. With a final effort he crawled closer to the tree, tangled the chain of his manacles in the limbs, gripped the trunk with his thighs and reached out to clasp Menas's outstretched hand.

"Pray for me, Zara," he gasped, surrendering his fate to God and the rushing torrent.

TURNING BLUE

The *Pravda* bobbed at anchor a safe distance from the peaceful shore. The island looked as idyllic as ever, apart from the ominous dust cloud hanging over the now barren cliffs. Earthquakes were one of the few things Zara had feared since her father told her of the phenomenon. Having now witnessed first-hand the awesome forces unleashed when the earth moved, terror had rendered her incapable of thought or movement.

She was aware the crew were waiting for her command to pull in to the island, but the prospect of setting foot on Zante conjured her Papa's warnings of aftershocks...

She startled when Jakov touched her elbow. "You must overcome your fear, Zara. For Kon's sake. If he's still alive, he won't last long without our help."

"How can he have survived?" she retorted, gesturing to the splintered wreckage on the beach. "It's evident there are no signs of life. If the earthquake didn't kill him, the storm surge…"

The words died in her grief-tightened throat.

Silent minutes passed before he spoke again. "I knew the moment my son's soul was taken into heaven," he told her, his voice hoarse with emotion. He pressed a clenched fist to his chest. "I felt the bond break." He took hold of her trembling hands. "You and Konrad share a bond. Look into your heart. It will sense if he is dead."

She gripped his warm hand, inhaled a ragged breath and closed her eyes.

"Tell me what you see," he said.

At first there was only the dark, disturbing image of a ship tossed against a cliff. First the *Feloz*, then the *Pravda*, then her beloved *Nunziata*. She cried out her anguish as one after another the vessels broke against the rock. Then another vision slowly intruded. She opened her eyes. "Chains. He's chained."

"Yes," Jakov replied patiently, "we expected he'd be chained on the ship."

She closed her eyes again, searching. The mist cleared. "No, he's chained to a tree."

"A tree?"

She nodded. "An olive tree."

"Mayhap he was enlisted to haul tar," Lupomari offered. "He'd have passed through the olive grove."

She frowned, not sure of what appeared next. "His feet are black."

Jakov pecked a kiss on her forehead. "Bravely done! We must search at the tarpits."

A different, more vivid image arose to rob her of breath. She opened her eyes wide and shook her head vigorously. "No. He has turned blue."

Jakov eyed her, clearly suspecting she had delved too deeply into the world of visions. "With cold?"

She laughed and turned to Rospo. "Kon Wolf has turned blue, my friend," she exclaimed.

"Ha!" he shouted, rushing off to man the tiller.

"Set a course for the west side of the island," she told the gaping Lupomari. "I know where he is."

~ ~ ~

The constant drip, drip of water woke Kon. The memory of the desperate effort to hold on to the tree slowly drifted into his wits. He absently rubbed the grit out of one eye and realized his chains still held him to the branches of the floating trunk. But where was he?

When he put his hand back in the water, it instantly turned blue. Startled, he hastily removed it, relieved to see the normal color return.

Fearing he was in some cavernous antechamber to heaven, or mayhap hell, he raised his aching head. Menas was still attached to the tree, but didn't seem to be awake. The parts of his body in the water were also blue, not black.

Kon had believed death came in a moment, but perhaps it was a slow process, a journey they hadn't yet completed. They were somewhere between life and death, a place where all men were made the same.

He risked peering into the clear depths, but couldn't see bottom. There appeared to be no ledges jutting from the sheer walls towering above him. Fear of drowning in the blue abyss constricted his throat, but if it was part of the journey...

Menas stirred and blinked open one eye.

"We're nearly there," Kon said hoarsely.

"Where?"

"Heaven, I hope."

Menas raised his head and looked at his hands in the water. "Nonsense. We're in the Blue Cave."

"Right. We are slowly turning blue. It must be a waterway to the Almighty."

Menas stared at him. "You've evidently suffered a blow to the head, Konrad. In your studies of religion did you ever read of a blue waterway to heaven?"

He hesitated, admitting the notion did sound foolish. "No, but..."

"Have your tarred feet turned blue?"

Kon twisted to look at his feet in the water. They were blue except for the black soles. "Huh!" was the only remark that came to mind.

A smile tugged at the corners of Menas's lips. "The torrent must have carried us to the other side of the southern tip of the island. It's where the Blue Cave is. Zara's father told me he brought her here once."

A certainty washed over him. The woman he loved had been in this very cave before and she was close now.

He filled his lungs. "Zara," he bellowed, "I'm in the Blue Cave."

"Not too loud," Menas admonished as the cavern echoed his shout. "The earthquake may have loosened parts of the ceiling."

Chastened, Kon looked up. "Mayhap we should steer the tree to the opening."

"If we venture beyond the cave, the tide may carry us out into the Ionian Sea and they'll never find us."

"You believe they are searching?"

"I'm confident they are, but I hope they come before nightfall. We might freeze to death in here."

~ ~ ~

The *Pravda's* rowboat was lowered to the tranquil sea. Rospo and Jakov climbed down the rope ladder.

From the deck, Zara looked across at the low opening of the cave she remembered from long ago. If her father had never brought her here, she wouldn't have known where to look for Kon. It was a miracle long in the making. "I don't see why I can't come," she shouted down to the two men.

Jakov looked up. "Look. Kon may be badly injured, or worse. We'll hope for the best, but we must be prepared."

She sensed their worry Kon might not be happy to see her, since she had caused his torment. "Do you have the blankets?" she asked, knowing full well they did.

"I have everything," Jakov replied, "including my trusty adze and chisel."

"I thought it was just an adze?"

He shrugged. "I added to my collection. Drosik isn't going to miss it."

CHAINED FOREVER

Kon drifted in and out of sleep, vaguely aware each time he woke that more and more of his body was turning blue. When the water chilled his manhood, it gradually dawned on him he was naked. "The torrent tore off my loincloth," he muttered.

"Mine too," Menas replied hoarsely. "I've got blue balls."

Kon glanced down at his groin, chuckling at the strange sight he beheld. "Me too," he exclaimed.

The dire situation suddenly struck him as hysterically funny. He wondered how many men appeared before God on the Day of Reckoning with such colorful...

Menas was barely visible in the growing darkness but he sensed his friend's scowl. "I can't stop laughing," he confessed.

"Sleep," Menas commanded. "The tree is becoming waterlogged. Mayhap if we are asleep when we drown it will be easier."

It was the first time he'd detected defeat and

resignation in his friend's voice. It jolted him out of his hysteria. He forced his chilled arms to move in the water, paddling the tree towards the dwindling light at the cave's mouth. "I don't plan to die here when Zara is close at hand."

Menas turned away. "Want to show off your blue balls, eh?"

Kon clenched his jaw. The staunch comrade who had seen him through many trials and saved his life more than once was succumbing to the madness of despair. He couldn't allow it. "Wake up. Help me," he urged, splashing water on Menas. "Paddle to the light."

The Nubian made a half-hearted effort to move one arm in the water. "No one is coming," he whispered.

Kon hit the surface with the flat of his hand, drenching his friend again and filling the cave with the sounds of splashing water. "Help me."

Menas raised his head. "Hush. Hush. Did you hear that?"

There was a trace of expectancy in the Nubian's voice. With difficulty, Kon steadied his breathing and listened.

The incessant dripping went on; the pounding of his own heart filled his ears. But on the still air came the unmistakable sound of oar blades dipped in water, their wooden shafts grinding on tholes. A man's voice echoed off the cave's ceiling. "Konrad...Konrad."

His joy threatened to choke him. "Over here," he managed hoarsely. "We're over here."

He narrowed his eyes as a shape loomed. A rowboat.

"Thank God," the voice said.

Kon peered up at the face grinning at him. "Jakov?"

"Aye, and Rospo. And I see you've a shipmate aboard your leafy vessel."

"His name is Menas, a fellow slave. Is Zara with you?"

Jakov hesitated. "No. She was afraid you might be angry."

Did he mean she was still in Termoli, or had she gone back to Venezia? And why would he be angry with her? Before he could put his thoughts into words, Jakov rushed on. "I see you are firmly attached to the tree. Safest is to tow you out of the cave and get those irons off on board the ship. Agreed?"

Menas evidently understood yet another language. "You are angels sent from God."

Rospo's unmistakable face appeared next over the side of the boat. Jaw clenched, he stretched out a hand holding a rope, but said nothing, his gaze fixed on the eerie water.

Kon wound the end of the rope around his frozen hand. "Ready."

Their rescuers pulled on the oars, dragging the tree towards the entrance of the cave.

Kon murmured a prayer of grateful thanks he had escaped death yet again. Had he been granted life in order to wed Zara? Or would he be punished for his disbelief? He fervently hoped when he was taken aboard the rescue ship, she would be there to welcome him back to life.

~ ~ ~

Digging her fingernails into the railing of the forecastle, Zara stared at the opening of the cave for so long in the gathering darkness, everything became blurry.

At first she wasn't sure if it was the rowboat she espied coming towards the *Pravda*, then her spirits plummeted when she counted only two men in the boat. "They haven't found him," she murmured to Lupomari who stood next to her. "I was certain."

The captain leaned forward, as if to see more clearly. "Don't lose hope yet. They are towing something."

She narrowed her eyes, trying to see what he had seen. "Is it a raft?"

He shook his head. "No. A tree, I think."

Hope raced in her heart, but impatience tugged. The rowers were fighting the incoming tide and seemed to be making no headway.

Lupomari called for hands to come to the aid of the rowboat as it finally bumped alongside. "There are two men lying on the tree," he exclaimed. "One of them black."

Black? Not Kon then.

A pulse throbbed in her throat. "Is it Kon?" she shouted down to Jakov.

Rospo's rare grin calmed her fears.

The man lying face down on the tree-raft slowly turned his head to look up and a thousand winged creatures fluttered in her belly. As long as she lived she would never forget the endearing sight of Kon's white backside glowing in the light of the rising moon.

~ ~ ~

His endurance at an end, and confident his rescue was in good hands, Kon lay still while Jakov and Rospo undertook the delicate process of untangling him and Menas from the raft. He sensed other members of the crew had taken to the water and were holding the tree in place, assisting with the task.

He had a vague notion the ship was the *Ragusa*, but couldn't reconcile in his weary mind how that could be.

Menas was hauled aboard the rowboat first, then helped up the rope ladder. The tree dipped alarmingly without his comrade's weight to balance it, but Kon remained calm, despite coming close to being submerged. The prospect of climbing the ladder was daunting, but the certainty it was Zara who had peered over the side and called his name renewed his strength.

His nakedness was of concern. He wanted Zara's first sight of his body to be...well, not like this, beaten, starved, smeared with tar and half-drowned. God in his bounty had been generous with his male endowments. The shrivelled appendage between his legs was far from impressive now.

Strong hands and encouraging voices got him safely into the rowboat. They steadied his hips as he clamped his trembling hands on either side of the rough rope ladder. Filled with apprehension and shivering with cold, he gritted his teeth, put one foot on the bottom rung and began the shaky climb. Jakov climbed right behind him, saying nothing, but keeping one hand on his back. He braced Kon's waist as Lupomari helped him over the side. Someone threw a warm blanket over his trembling shoulders. He gathered it tightly to his body, teeth chattering, eyes searching desperately for one person.

Finally, he saw her standing nearby. Uncharacteristically hesitant. Was it true she feared his wrath? She looked so bereft, he wanted to reassure her, but he had to be sure she loved him, even at his worst. He opened his arms as wide as the chain allowed and spoke her name. "Zara."

She stooped beneath the chain, put her arms around his waist, pressed her body to his and sobbed on his shoulder. He folded the blanket around her and nuzzled his nose in her hair, inhaling deeply of Zara's unique aroma.

Salt, sea, woman.

He gently tightened the chain, pulling her closer. "You are mine, and I will never let you go," he growled.

Her warmth chased away the chill. His *rute* stirred pleasantly, putting a welcome end to any worries on that score. His knees were of greater concern. "I need to sit," he said hoarsely, "and I am getting you wet."

Her eyes brimming with tears, she leaned back again the restraint, pressing her hips to his arousal. She folded the blanket back around him and raked his wet hair off his face. "Hear my confession first," she whispered. "My pigheadedness was the cause of your suffering."

"I love your pigheadedness," he replied, holding onto her shoulders for support, filled with a comforting premonition he would always be able to rely on her strength.

She fisted her hands in the blanket. "And I

love you. Now you must rest. The men will help you to the bed we've readied."

Certain now of her love, his confidence in the future blossomed. Zara was indeed the grail he'd been seeking. She and a black man he'd encountered by chance had helped him rediscover who he was. "Is Menas the Nubian safe?" he asked as two crewmen took him by the arms.

She stepped back under the chain. "Menas?"

"My comrade."

"The man rescued with you is Menas of Nubia?"

"Yes. He saved my life more than once."

She looked at him curiously. "He was a partner in several of my father's African business ventures."

"He told me he knew your father. It was he kept the hope alive that you would come."

"My father described him as a man of great faith, but it cannot be him."

"Why not?"

"He died three years ago."

A SORRY TALE

Kon took Zara's hand. "I admit there were times when I thought I had lost my wits, but I can assure you my comrade *is* Menas of Nubia. Come with me and you'll see."

Buoyed by the strength of his calloused grasp, even after his ordeal, she went willingly as the crewmen helped him walk to beneath the stern-castle.

She had met Menas once when she was a young girl, and wasn't sure if the haggard black man crouched on the hides and shrouded in blankets was indeed her father's friend. His gaze was fixed on the adze and chisel Jakov was wielding in an effort to break apart one leg shackle. Shattered manacles already lay nearby.

He looked up as she and Kon approached. His broad smile dispelled any doubts. "Zara Polani," he chuckled. "You were a child the last time I saw you. Look at you now. Konrad is a lucky man."

Confused and flustered, she watched as her grinning lover was lowered to the hides, then fell to her knees between him and his comrade, her hand still in Kon's grasp. "I don't understand. My father thought you were dead."

He winced as the shackle broke apart, then wrapped his long fingers around his liberated ankle. "In a way I was. I was kidnapped by slavers and taken to Egypt. You may be aware Nubia supplies the Fatimids with a large number of their slave soldiers. I'm ashamed to admit I myself once traded men to them." He shook his head. "Never again, I assure you."

"Amen," Kon replied.

"But you disappeared three years ago," Zara protested.

Menas stretched out his other ankle for Jakov. "I served in the Mamluk army for almost two."

"Two years," Kon exclaimed, his eyes on Jakov's progress. "I'd have gone mad."

Menas nodded. "I was fortunate. My commander was a kind, devout man. Kareem of Alexandria."

"A Mohammedan?" Kon asked.

Menas frowned. "Do not make the mistake of assuming all who are faithful to Islam are monsters like Nizar. It was Kareem who helped me escape."

"Why?"

He leaned back on his elbows and braced

himself as the remaining leg shackle fell way after one last blow from Jakov. "You must understand. The Fatimids view their slave armies as a means of providing security not only for their caliphate but for the men in those armies. They are slaves, yes, but their needs are met—good food, clothing, shelter, even wives. They have status and are allowed to carry weapons. Most of them are better off than they would have been had they not been conscripted into the army."

Kon scoffed. "Benevolent slavery."

"In a way," Menas agreed, accepting a tumbler of ale from a crewman. "But it preyed on Kareem's mind that I was a successful trader who had brought wealth not only to myself, but to my country. My enslavement was detrimental to Nubia in his view because I was no longer of value to my fellow Nubians, Christian and Mohammedan. He regarded it as a sin."

Zara had doubts. "He freed you, though he was aware you were a Christian?"

He took a long draught of the ale. "As I told Kon, Islam and Christianity have co-existed in peace in Nubia for generations. My faith was of no importance to Kareem. My stature humbled him. He risked much in freeing me, but an opportunity arose during a campaign against the Berbers in Tripolitania."

"In Libya?" Kon asked, splaying his hands flat as Jakov made ready to break his manacles. Zara missed the security of his grip.

Menas scratched under his chin. "Too anxious to return to Nubia, I made an error in judgement. I hired on as a crew member of a ship bound for Alexandria. I believed the Coptic Patriarch would grant me sanctuary and help me get back to my homeland."

She helped Kon sip his ale while Jakov tackled his restraints. "What happened?"

"The Mediterranean can be treacherous. We were caught in a violent storm and carried far from shore. The boat broke apart. I would have drowned but for another Mohammedan, a crew member who helped me cling to a piece of wreckage for hours."

Zara had a dreadful premonition. "You washed ashore in Italy."

"Indeed. We were discovered half dead on a beach by peasants. They recognized their good fortune in stumbling upon two black men and sold us to our friend Nizar."

She frowned when Kon choked on his ale. This was the second mention of the name. "Nizar?"

Menas shook his head. "Don't ask."

"What happened to your companion? The one who saved you?"

Menas clenched his jaw. "I watched him die in the stinking hull of the *Feloz* after Nizar's henchmen cut out his tongue. I was powerless to do anything to aid him."

Zara trembled as Kon and Menas stared silently into the hell they'd shared, the only sound the metallic thud of the adze as it struck the chisel.

She accepted that the man she loved might never reveal to her what had happened aboard the slave ship. She made a solemn vow to fill his remaining days with a love so fierce and all-consuming that the horrors he'd endured would fade into a forgotten memory.

Kon had faltered before under the weight of adversity and sorrow. But now he had Zara Polani to share his burdens and she looked forward with relish to the challenge.

OLIVES

Three days later Kon stood with his arm around Zara's waist on the forecastle of the *Pravda* as Jakov guided the cog into Bari under the watchful eye of Lupomari. The rechristening of the *Ragusa* seemed to have expunged the horrific memories of his confinement, though he still preferred to keep his eyes averted from the thwarts.

Disaster seemed to stalk him in the port town, yet he looked forward to their arrival, aware of Zara's nervous excitement.

It was the first day he'd been strong enough to remain on his feet for more than an hour and he wanted to share in her joy when she set eyes on her beloved flagship again.

She'd fussed over him during the entire voyage from Zante. Before they left the stricken island, Rospo had insisted on undertaking an excursion onshore. They supposed he intended to search for survivors, but he returned with the news he had found only death and destruction. However, the crewmen who accompanied him carried handfuls of olives. He gave Zara a terse explanation. "Tar."

Apparently, a five year acquaintance with the man had given her insights into his thoughts, and she understood at once. The oily fruit would help soften the hardened tar.

She pitted and mashed the olives then patiently bathed the soles of his feet and his back with repeated applications of the stuff.

He experienced a ridiculous surge of jealousy when she daubed the mush on Menas's back, feeling especially foolish when his grinning friend shot him a mocking wink.

Slowly, the tar came off, the last of it removed by a gentle rubbing with a holystone. He'd been sceptical, but having the soles of his feet massaged with the rough stone turned out to be an arousing experience.

He tucked the revelation away for the future.

He lusted for her as much as he ever did— mayhap more now he was sure she was his. However, he'd learned patience and was reconciled to waiting for what they both desired —to surrender their virginity to each other in a sweet-smelling bed as man and wife.

It was what his parents would have expected of him. The certainty of it led him to a decision. "After we dock," he whispered in her ear, "and you and Lupomari have hugged and kissed your beloved *Nunziata...* "

"Don't forget Rospo," she interrupted with feigned seriousness.

"And Rospo," he conceded. "Then we must go to the Venetian church you told me of."

"I intended for us to go there. They will be relieved you are safe."

"Good. I need to beg the services of a scrivener and the means for a missive to be sent to Wolfenberg in the hope my father is still alive. It may be many months before I can travel to Saxony and I want him to know I am safe and well."

She stood on tiptoe and kissed his cheek. "Will you tell him about me?"

He circled her waist and pulled her to his body. "If I had the ability to conjure some alchemy to spirit us both to Saxony this moment, I would. My Papa will love you."

The kiss he planned to bestow on her tempting lips was thwarted by a shout from Rospo. *"Nun-zee-ata,"* he sang from the stern-castle as if he'd set eyes on a long lost lover.

"We can't go at this moment," she replied, wriggling with excitement in his arms, straining to catch a first glimpse of her ship.

~ ~ ~

The Venetians of Bari welcomed the travellers warmly and offered accommodations in the *dormitorios.* A smith was located who carefully removed the neck collars Jakov had been unwilling to tackle with his adze.

Kon dictated a letter to a scrivener and Lupomari found a captain who undertook to take it as far as Genoa then pass it on to traders heading north into Germany.

They lingered a fortnight to give Kon and Menas time to recover from their ordeal, and to prepare both ships for a long voyage. Zara's intention was to spend time securing a cargo for the *Nunziata* to transport to Venezia, but the opportunity to spend time with Kon won out. She left the task in the capable hands of Lupomari and his crew.

Jakov had been persuaded to sail the *Pravda* to the republic before going on to Croatia. At first he'd been reluctant to agree to her urgings that he take his case against the Venetian slavers to the Doge, claiming he and his men simply wanted to get home.

However, the invitation to attend a wedding eventually convinced him.

He spent most of his time on the docks with his men and they saw little of him during the day.

She and Kon and Menas strolled in the church's quiet courtyard, enjoying the late afternoon sunshine. Born into different cultures, they shared tales of their lives before they met.

She had never candidly discussed Bruno with anyone before, not even Ottavia, who barely acknowledged she had a brother. Strangely, she was at ease telling the two men of the joys and difficulties of having a grown brother with the mind of a child. She admitted often being more at odds with her younger sister.

Menas spoke with pride about Nubia and the fertile valley of the River Nile. Folk eyed them curiously when Kon and Zara tried to follow the steps of a traditional Nubian dance he demonstrated. Or mayhap the loud chanting caught their attention.

Kon talked at length of his family, especially of his English-born mother, and Zara sensed he had become reconciled to her loss.

It was gratifying to see both men regain their strength, and she marvelled neither had lost his sense of humor. Indeed, Kon seemed to have acquired a mature serenity. The impetuous intensity was gone. The fires of hell had forged a man of the strongest steel.

Yet he wasn't afraid to show his emotions, as evidenced by their parting with Menas on the fourteenth day. Lupomari had arranged passage for him on a reputable ship with an experienced captain, another Nubian. "Let us hope I make it safely to Alexandria this time," he quipped.

Splendid in flowing new robes of gold and purple purchased from African traders in the market, Menas had a kind word and a farewell embrace for everyone—the captain, Jakov, even Rospo. He bestowed a courtly kiss on Zara's hand and finally faced Kon. No words were exchanged. The two men who had helped each other survive unspeakable hardship simply embraced for long, silent minutes until Menas broke away and strode up the gangplank of the waiting ship.

Kon put an arm around Zara's waist and raised a hand in salute as the cog was shoved away from the dock. "Go with God, my friend," he shouted in a voice hoarse with emotion.

Menas waved back. "God is always with me," he replied with a bright smile.

WELCOME TO VENEZIA

Fair winds prevailed throughout the voyage from Bari to Venezia. Zara took it as a good omen. She loved being at sea, but was overjoyed to reach home port. It meant a reunion with the man she loved who had sailed as steersman on the *Pravda* while she had remained aboard the *Nunziata*.

The separation had been Kon's suggestion. She'd missed him more than she thought possible, but accepted it was for the best. Five days in close quarters on the same ship with no opportunity for privacy would have been worse than exchanging an occasional distant wave across the watery expanse between the two ships.

When the *Nunziata* pulled into the lagoon, it was evident from the loud cheers of men on the docks that news of their adventures had already reached Venezia. Her crew added to the hubbub when they disembarked and shared tales of the voyage with welcoming comrades. "I suppose I shouldn't be surprised," she remarked to Lupomari. "I've always said nothing goes on anywhere in the four corners of the earth that the republic's ships don't report back in short order."

The captain stroked his beard, looking to the far end of the dock. "However, you probably didn't expect this."

She followed his gaze, recognizing her uncle's devise emblazoned on the tunics of three soldiers marching towards them. Those in their path quickly stepped aside when they caught sight of the winged golden lion of San Marco.

The three came to an abrupt halt when they reached the *Nunziata* and eyed the gangplank with nervous hesitation. She would have been amused at their fear had it not been a distraction from watching the *Pravda* dock nearby. She thirsted to reunite with Kon, but couldn't ignore a delegation from the Doge.

She gripped the railing of the forecastle and called to them. "I am Zara Polani. You are welcome to come aboard."

She normally took perverse pleasure in asserting her authority over men, but their scowls only served to increase her irritation. She folded her arms and stared, her foot tapping loudly on the planking.

One of the soldiers evidently decided to take

the lead, though all three remained on the dock. "*Signorina* Polani, it is you we seek," he declared. "Our beloved Doge sends his regards and wishes to welcome you home."

A summons from the Doge, uncle or no, had to be obeyed, but when she espied Kon hurrying along the dock, she smiled and decided this was as good a time as any to introduce Pietro Polani to his future nephew-by-marriage.

~ ~ ~

The voyage to Venezia provided Kon with many hours to ponder his experiences in the sennights since he'd sailed away on the *Nunziata*.

He was a man reborn from the ashes of his former self. It had never been part of God's plan that he become a priest. The fateful beating and consequent humiliation suffered in Bari, the rockfall, even the horrendous suffering aboard the *Feloz*, all had been part of the journey he was meant to take to his true destiny—Zara.

He'd been provided with guardian angels; his family, especially his father who had allowed him to wander; Menas, the safe harbor in a sea of despair. He'd been tested by the malevolent forces of Drosik and Nizar, and Duke Heinrich. Now the pilgrimage was almost complete. The one important step remaining was to wed the woman he loved.

He disembarked as soon as the *Pravda* was safely moored and hurried along the docks to reunite with Zara. He became concerned when he espied three soldiers with the Doge's devise on their tunics at the foot of the gangplank of the *Nunziata*. Her enthusiastic wave from the forecastle reassured him, but he paused, able now to think before he reacted. The appearance of these men reminded him there was yet unfinished business. A wrong to be righted.

He resumed his pace and reached the gangplank. "I am Konrad Dieter von Wolfenberg of Saxony, *Signorina* Polani's betrothed," he announced proudly. "State your business."

The three wrinkled their noses and eyed his sailor's garb, but it was evident from the puzzled looks on their faces his manner of speech had confused them.

The soldier who appeared to be in charge straightened the front of his tunic. "His Excellency the Doge requests his niece's presence at the palace."

Kon glanced up at Zara. Her amused smile and nod of approval indicated she had an inkling of what he planned to say. "Then I will accompany her."

~ ~ ~

A thrill of anticipation swirled through Zara's veins. She was a successful woman of commerce who made decisions normally made by men. Fate had cast her in the role. Many resented her authoritative manner; Kon recognised it as a strength. He would never be afraid to challenge her but she was confident he didn't seek to dominate her. She looked forward to trading wits with him.

She had to accept she wouldn't always get her way, as she had in the past, but ceding to Kon would be no hardship. Her heart was irrevocably lost the moment she first set eyes on him.

She strode proudly down the gangplank and accepted his hand when she reached the dock. "Welcome to Venezia, Konrad von Wolfenberg."

His answering smile and the light brush of his lips across her knuckles sent desire spiralling up her thighs. "I thank you, *Signorina* Polani, and it will be my honor to accompany you to your uncle's palace. However, I am of the opinion Count Jakov of Istria should also attend the audience."

The soldiers looked from one to the other, clearly confused.

"I agree," she replied with a wink, enjoying

the ease with which they both fell into the role, as if they'd been friends for a long time.

"Follow us to the count's ship," he instructed the soldiers in a manner that reminded her he'd once been an officer in the imperial army. She was probably the only one who noticed his nose twitching slightly in the endearing way she loved.

She stifled the urge to laugh as the soldiers quickly shuffled into line and followed them to the *Pravda*.

~ ~ ~

"Relations with my uncle Pietro have been strained since my father's death," Zara confided to Kon and Jakov.

They had been instructed to wait in an elaborately gilded antechamber of the Council Room at the *Palazzo Ducale*. She'd grown up surrounded by wealth, but the chamber suddenly struck her as garishly over-decorated. She wondered what Kon thought of it as he gazed around, nose twitching more than usual.

"Why?" Jakov asked.

"As I explained, my brother is incapable and I believe my uncle expected the Polani fleet to come to him."

"But your father had other ideas," Kon said. "He recognized you were the one to take control. A wise man indeed."

She preened, recognizing how fortunate she
was to have found a lover who wasn't
threatened by her abilities. "In any event, my
uncle is richer than Croesus. Poor men don't
get elected Doge of Venezia."

He raised his eyes to the mural on the ceiling.
"I can see."

"I don't envy him," Jakov said. "From what I
understand, he cannot leave this palace."

She nodded. "Only to go to the chapel, the
Basilica di San Marco, the edifice next door."

"Rather like being a slave," Kon remarked.

"But an extremely powerful one," she
reminded them as the double doors opened
slowly and they stepped inside. "It's wise not to
forget it."

To his credit, when he noticed her attire, her
uncle hesitated only a moment before rising
from his ornate chair and spreading his arms
wide. "Zara, my child," he gushed.

She had no memory of ever being embraced
by him, but went into his arms after a brief and
not well-executed curtsey. "*Zio*," she whispered,
swallowing the lump in her throat when a
memory of her Papa surfaced.

He put his hands on her shoulders and held
her away. The genuine concern in his grey eyes
threw her off balance. "Let me be sure you are
well. Outrageously garbed as usual. I am

hearing tales of piracy and enslavement."

She took a deep breath. "I will gladly tell the whole story when we are more presentable, but permit me to introduce the man I am going to marry, Konrad von Wolfenberg."

Konrad stepped forward, bowed and held out his hand. "Your Grace, I am honored to meet you."

She'd wager her betrothed wasn't what he expected. Nevertheless, he accepted Kon's hand. "Welcome, I take it from your speech you are not from Venezia."

"I'm a Saxon," he replied, "the son of Count Dieter von Wolfenberg."

She suspected from her uncle's wide-eyed stare that for once he'd been taken by surprise.

"The renowned diplomat?"

"He's the one," he answered proudly, "and it seems I have inherited his belief in the need for justice. May I introduce our companion, Jakov, Count of Istria."

Jakov bowed. "Your Grace."

Her uncle frowned. "Istria? A neighbor."

"Indeed," Kon declared. "Yet this high-ranking nobleman and his son were kidnapped by Venetians and sold into slavery. He escaped, but not before his heir drowned. As Chief Magistrate of the Republic, you'll agree, Your Grace, that this crime cannot go unpunished."

Pride soared in Zara's veins as she witnessed the transformation in Kon's demeanor. He was no longer a troubled, impetuous young man. The confident, assertive nobility instilled in him since birth had resurfaced.

It was humbling to think her love had played a part in his rebirth.

Her uncle stiffened his shoulders. She half-expected he would seek confirmation of Kon's allegations from her, but instead he spoke to Jakov.

"We apologise for this unforgivable attack on your person, Count, and we grieve the loss of your son. Please remain when the others leave us and we will discuss the matter further. Return on the morrow, Zara, and we will make preparations for your wedding with my chancellor."

Kon bowed. She curtseyed. He proffered his arm and they left the chamber, only pausing to embrace once the double doors had closed behind them.

"You were magnificent," she said with a smile. "Now to meet my family."

BRUNO

As he and Zara entered the Polani apartments adjacent to the palace, Kon admitted inwardly he was nervous at the prospect of being introduced to her brother and sister. During his interview with the Doge, he'd been confident and assertive. It was as if he'd suddenly metamorphosed into his father.

Siblings were a different matter. He had first hand experience, but none of his brothers were mentally deficient, despite Johann's fears he might inherit his birth mother's madness. He'd never heard Sophia utter a single word of sarcasm. "I hope they like me," he whispered lamely.

She squeezed his hand and smiled, but he got the feeling she was also unsure of their reception.

When they entered the solar, Ottavia rushed to embrace Zara. "Sister," she exclaimed. "I have been frantic."

As they broke apart both women seemed surprised and somewhat embarrassed by the obvious affection that had passed between them. He was confident his reunion with his kin would be less strained.

Zara straightened her tunic and linked her arm in his. "This is Kon, my betrothed."

Her introduction seemed informal. Nevertheless, he clicked his heels like the disciplined Saxon officer he was and bowed smartly. "*Signorina* Ottavia."

He straightened and took hold of her outstretched hand. A fleeting but unmistakable glint of disdain flashed in her eyes as she inspected his garb.

"Welcome to our family," she said without warmth as he brushed a polite kiss on her knuckles. "I see my sister has found a fellow sailor to wed."

Zara smiled like a contented cat. "Konrad is from Saxony," she revealed. "The son of Count Dieter von Wolfenberg."

Ottavia's demeanor changed. She smiled brightly. "Oh! In that case..."

Zara laughed. "You're such a snob, sister dear," she taunted.

Kon feared an argument might ensue. However, the door opened unexpectedly and a young man entered in the company of an elderly gentleman who reminded him of one of Sophia's former music teachers.

Zara opened her arms wide. "Bruno!"

If she hadn't spoken his name, he would have known the lanky young man was her brother. He could pass for her twin. He bounded across the chamber into her embrace, laughing and sobbing at the same time. "Missed Zara," he said over and over as she stroked his hair, her eyes welling tears.

Ottavia looked on, fists clenched at her sides, her mouth drawn into a tight line. She was clearly embarrassed and he'd wager Bruno didn't get much affection from his youngest sister.

When he calmed, Zara took him by the hand and led him to Kon. "I am getting married, brother dearest. This man is my betrothed, Konrad."

Bruno studied his feet for long moments, rocking back and forth.

Unsure if he should speak, Kon looked to Zara, but she shook her head.

"We love each other," she explained. "He will be a brother for you."

Bruno raised his head and stared at Kon with emerald eyes he recognised.

Kon smiled and stretched out his hand. "Hello, Bruno."

Bruno stepped forward abruptly and threw his arms around him. "Kon-rad," he stammered.

"Bro-ther."

Kon choked back tears as he returned the hearty embrace.

A VENETIAN WEDDING

"Three stages must be observed in a Venetian wedding," Zara explained to Kon as they walked with Jakov to her uncle's council chambers. "The first step involves the families of the bride and groom drawing up the agreement. Normally, the bride doesn't need to be there, but I have no intention of leaving decisions regarding our future to my uncle."

"Hopefully, Jakov can act as my sponsor," he replied, "since my family is in Germany."

She paused outside the doors and smoothed her hands over the brocade of his new black and gold tunic. "The tailors did an outstanding job with this garment in the few short hours they had available. You look handsome."

"What about me?" Jakov preened playfully, puffing out his chest.

She rolled her eyes. "You look wonderful too, but I am not marrying you."

It was the first time she'd seen the new clothing. Her uncle had insisted Kon and Jakov lodge at the palace, not in her family apartments, and she'd reluctantly concurred it was more appropriate.

The doors opened and they were ushered inside by her uncle's chamberlain. To her surprise, several members of the advisory council were also in attendance. She was pleased when her uncle introduced Kon with obvious pride, explaining the noble dynasty from which he was descended. She hadn't known one of his ancestors had fought for William the Conqueror at the Battle of Hastings and been declared a hero. The Doge had evidently been asking questions.

When Jakov was introduced, no mention of his kidnapping ordeal was made, but it was evident the Croat seemed comfortable. She surmised their discussions had gone well, and hoped for justice for him before he sailed home.

The scrivener slowly explained the contents of the documents spread out on the enormous council table. She noted her uncle had made no mention of the Polani ships. "This has to be changed," she declared. "My husband will be designated Bruno's guardian with oversight for the fleet. His name must also be added to my brother's will as his sole heir."

"It's not necessary," Kon protested quietly.

She drew him aside. "You will be my partner

in all things," she insisted, avoiding her uncle's glare, "then there will be no question regarding our children's inheritance."

He nodded his understanding.

Her uncle sulked while the scrivener shuffled the parchments and made the changes, but neither he nor the *sapientes* voiced any objection.

Zara read over the documents a second time and offered them to Kon. "You should check them. They're in Latin."

He shook his head. "I can read Latin, but I have complete faith in your judgement."

Zara had penned her signature to many documents, but never had as much confidence in any of them as she did in the agreement binding her to Kon.

He added his signature with a flourish. "I want to kiss you, but I sense our audience wouldn't approve," he whispered under his breath.

Jakov acted as a witness. Her uncle signed and added his seal. When he pecked a kiss on her cheek the dignitaries applauded briefly and then paraded out, leaving her with Kon and Jakov.

Kon took her hand. "What's the next step in a Venetian wedding?"

"On the morrow comes the *fidanzamento*—the betrothal," she explained.

"I'm confused. Isn't that what we just accomplished?"

She hesitated. Evidently things were done differently in Saxony. "In Venezia, at the betrothal we exchange simple vows, and… gifts."

"What kind of gifts?"

"A piece of fruit, a token, a ring sometimes."

He turned to Jakov. "You and I need to busy ourselves finding a gift for me to give to my lovely bride."

"No need," she replied too quickly, feeling unexpectedly shy. "Often the gift is a kiss."

He wiggled his eyebrows. "I can fulfill such a requirement."

The chamber was suddenly stiflingly hot. She wished Jakov wasn't present. "And the kiss usually leads to…er…"

Their Croatian friend grinned. "*Consummation* is the word she's looking for."

~ ~ ~

In the event, the *fidanzamento* was delayed for a sennight in order to allow for preparations for the betrothal banquet. Having learned he and Zara would finally join their bodies after the ceremony, Kon chafed that such a long interval was necessary, but she insisted he would understand once the festivities began.

Considering it had taken only a day to make

his new tunic, he deemed the lengthy sessions with the tailors tedious. Zara too spent hours being measured and fitted for her gown. While he eagerly looked forward to seeing her in something other than leggings, it seemed a waste of time since he intended they be rid of their clothing at the earliest opportunity.

He was appreciative of the chance to assist Jakov with readying the *Pravda* for the voyage to Croatia. It helped take his mind off the constant daydreaming of seeing his beautiful lover naked for the first time.

He and Jakov were summoned to the council chambers in the palace several times to add to their testimony regarding the Venetian slavers who had carried out the kidnapping, but were given no indication as to any progress in the investigation. It dismayed him that Jakov wasn't hopeful.

When the afternoon of the banquet arrived, he awaited his bride in the Doge's solar, rehearsing over and over what he would be expected to say.

"Be calm," Jakov urged.

Kon ceased pacing. "I used to easily memorize long passages from the Greek philosophers but suddenly I can barely remember a few simple words."

"Don't worry. Zara will be so impressed with

your outfit, she won't notice if you make a slip. The woman is smitten with you anyway."

There was an unmistakable hint of melancholy in his friend's voice and it struck him he knew little about Jakov. "It was remiss of me. I never enquired if you have a wife."

The count averted his gaze. "Tatjana died in childbirth."

Kon fiddled with the cuffs of his tunic, suspecting Jakov wouldn't wish to further discuss such a sorrowful event. "I have to admit the tailors did a fine job," he said lamely.

Fashioned of the finest Tuscan wool, the calf length blue tunic and the leggings were a perfect fit. He felt almost regal in the red mantle trimmed with squirrel and fastened on one shoulder. He was more than suitably attired, but his mouth fell open when Zara entered on her uncle's arm. The red of her ankle-length gown matched his cloak, though it was made of lighter material, probably silk. The high neck revealed nothing of her bosom, but the fitted bodice emphasized the tempting curve of her breasts. The sleeves were tight from shoulder to elbow, then flared out into a trumpet shape. A corded girdle of blue circled her waist, the tasseled ends resting alluringly atop her mons.

He'd never seen anything as stylish in

Saxony. Indeed, he'd never set eyes on a more stunning bride. And she was his!

"My lady," he whispered, proffering his arm.

"My lord," she replied with a smile, raking her eyes over his outfit.

The Doge and his duchess led the procession. Feeling like Paris with Helen of Troy on his arm, Kon escorted Zara into the Grand Hall of the *Palazzo Ducale*.

~ ~ ~

Zara walked proudly into the Grand Hall on Kon's arm, remembering vividly the fleeting vision she'd had in the sheltered bay at Scardovari. Had Fate brought them together?

She'd long been proud of her ability to operate the fleet without the help of a man, but truth be told she had given up hope of ever finding a helpmate who wasn't simply interested in marrying into the Polani family. Kon was her miracle. Power and prestige meant nothing to him.

When she'd mentioned Bruno didn't attend public events, he'd enquired as to the reason. She admitted it was to avoid embarrassment and agreed he should be present. When she caught sight of her brother's angelically happy face in the crowd, she was filled with regret that he had been excluded from so many important occasions. It was evident the folk around him were enjoying his child-like pleasure as much as he was.

As usual, Ottavia was the most lavishly dressed woman in the entire crowd. She wore a green silk concoction which had probably cost more than the wedding gown, but she seemed to be genuinely glad for Zara. If only she would stop making eyes at Jakov. Did she seriously believe a man like him would be interested in a spiteful…

She pushed aside the negative thoughts and soaked up the gasps of delight from the richly attired nobles and ladies invited to the banquet, smiling indulgently. A hush fell when they took their places at the front of the head table where they were joined by the Patriarch of Venezia. Bruno suddenly squealed with laughter and clapped his hands, but his outburst calmed her rapidly beating heart.

At a prearranged signal from the cleric, Kon took hold of her hands, inhaled deeply and asked, "Will you wed with me, Zara Polani?"

"I will," she replied without hesitation, sure in her heart he was the right man. "Will you wed with me, Konrad Dieter von Wolfenberg?"

"I will," he vowed. "I will."

The Patriarch intoned a lengthy blessing in Latin.

Everyone responded with a loud *Amen*, then

loud cheering broke out. Bruno rushed forward to hug first her then Kon, his obvious joy eliciting sentimental oohs and aahs and thunderous applause from the guests.

"That's it?" Kon shouted over the din after Ottavia, of all people, had escorted their brother back to his place. "You're my wife now?"

"I am."

He took her into his embrace and pulled her to his body. They kissed, deeply, passionately, without regard for the cheering and whistling audience. Their tongues mated; they shared breath, tasting each other.

They broke apart when her smiling uncle clapped his hands and invited them to take their places next to him at the head table.

Servers spilled out of the kitchens carrying platters laden with food. Kon rubbed his hands together. "I am anxious to taste what took a sennight to prepare."

His twitching nose brought home to her how much she loved his boyish enthusiasm. After everything he'd endured...

"The dishes will be delicious, but bear in mind the cooks had to make sufficient food for three days of feasting."

"Three days? I thought..."

He looked so crestfallen, she had to enlighten

him. "Don't worry. You and I aren't expected to stay for the whole time."

He took hold of her hand and leaned over to whisper in her ear. "Be forewarned, I will get my revenge for your teasing."

She marvelled that something as ordinary as the touch of another person's skin and the warmth of his breath on her ear could cause such delicious sensations of aching need in private places. "I can't wait."

He shifted his weight on the chair. "If I was to put your hand on a certain part of my body..."

Waves of heat threatened to turn her skin the same color as her gown, but a serving wench placed food before them and he let go of her hand.

He unfastened his cloak and a servant appeared as if by magic to carry it away.

She fluttered her eyelashes. "Are you feeling the heat too, Konrad Wolf?"

"Minx," he growled.

He turned his attention to his trencher, a quizzical look on his face. "Pastries for the first course?"

"Made with pine nuts, and almonds," she explained. "They whet the appetite."

He chuckled after sampling one. "My appetite has already been whetted. Mmm. Tastes like marzipan."

He licked his fingers when the second course was served. "Aha! Sausages and meatballs. More like Saxon food."

She simply nodded as he bit into a meatball, her mind still on offering to lick his sticky fingers.

"Spicier than at home," he said. "But good."

His remark troubled her. "I was hoping you would consider Venezia as your home now."

He looked into her eyes. "My home is wherever you are, Zara. I have no land or title waiting for me in Saxony, but I hope one day we will travel there together. I want to take you to my homeland and show you off to my family."

She leaned forward to kiss his lips, to the delight of the guests whose lusty cheers only served to make the heat rise in her face again. "I would love to visit Saxony with you. Too bad we can't go by sea!"

He chuckled and bit into a small sausage.

"There's a lot more food to come," she warned. "Roasted partridge, capons, ham, pigeons, wild boar. And that's only today's fare."

He dabbed his mouth with a napkin, his eyes dark. "Aboard the *Feloz*, I feared I might never taste good food again."

She couldn't meet his anguished gaze. "Forgive me."

He tucked his finger under her chin and raised her face to look at him. "There is nothing to forgive. I would gladly sacrifice myself again for your happiness." His frown turned to a broad grin. "And to that end I will force myself to eat whatever is put in front of me this day. I need my strength for the strenuous night ahead."

She couldn't help it. She laughed out loud, drawing the curious eye of many in the hall.

MISCHIEF AFOOT

The feasting and drinking carried on for hours. Kon had no trouble keeping pace with the food, but only sipped the rich Tuscan wine imbibed by many in startling quantities.

Several of the male guests stood, one after another, and led suggestive chants that became more lewd as the afternoon turned into evening. When everyone else had echoed their verse to their satisfaction, they sat and were rewarded with raucous laughter and applause.

"Reminds me of the *reigen* Lute is fond of," he told Zara.

"A Saxon tradition?"

"A chain dance with a leader who chants a verse the dancers echo. My brother's *reigen* at weddings tended to get more bawdy as time went on, though excessive drink wasn't the reason. He just likes to have fun."

She put a hand on his knee. "You miss your family."

He covered her hand with his own. "I wish they were here to share in my happiness, but my brothers would be plotting mischief, at our expense."

Her eyes widened. "Such as?"

He chuckled at the memories. "When my sister got married, Lute and I let live rabbits loose in the bridal chamber."

"Rabbits! I'll wager her husband wasn't happy."

"No, and trust me it was no easy task corralling those timid creatures in order to release them into the chamber at the right moment. However, Brandt got his revenge on Lute."

"I am afraid to ask."

"He tied cowbells underneath the bed when my brother married Francesca."

Giddy with laughter, she looked around the hall. "Merry as these guests are, I don't foresee any of them playing those kinds of pranks." She rolled her eyes. "They would be considered most inappropriate in the *Palazzo Ducale.*"

He kissed her hand. "You sense I miss their mischief-making. I love you for it."

She blushed as he gazed into her emerald eyes. "It's time you gave me my gift," she said in the sultriest voice he had ever heard.

"I've had it ready for a while," he teased. "What's the protocol for leaving?"

She came to her feet. "Don't worry. They

won't notice we are gone."

He stood and took her by the hand. "And where are we going?"

She grinned. "To the ducal bridal chamber of course."

~ ~ ~

Their exit didn't go unnoticed. They were almost through the doors when Ottavia came running across the hall, shrieking for them to wait. An icy shiver marched across Zara's nape. Astonished at this uncharacteristic behavior, she paused to inform her sister in no uncertain terms she didn't want or require her company. The words died in her throat when she realized Ottavia had Bruno in tow.

Kon's grip on her hand tightened. "Stay calm," he advised, though she sensed a slight impatience in his tone.

She settled a false grin on her face. "I have prayed one day Ottavia would acknowledge she has a brother, but does it have to be today?"

Bruno outpaced his younger sister and launched himself at Kon and Zara, nigh on knocking them off balance. "Come too," he shouted.

Panting, Ottavia caught up. Zara couldn't recall ever seeing her sister blush, but there was no mistaking the red flush that crept up her neck and spread across her barely covered breasts when Jakov appeared at her side.

"Surely you're not leaving without saying goodnight?" the Croat teased.

Ottavia giggled.

Giggled!

Kon clenched his jaw and glared at his friend. "I was about to give my bride her long-awaited gift," he growled.

Ottavia linked her arm with Kon. "We'll see you safely to the chamber, won't we, Count Jakov?"

"Indeed we will," he echoed with a wink, taking Zara by the arm.

"Me, me," Bruno insisted.

Zara recognised it would pointless to argue. "Looks like I was wrong," she whispered to Kon. "Mayhap there is some mischief afoot."

~ ~ ~

Kon couldn't deny he was irritated by the unexpected trio tagging along, but it was of some consolation that he was no longer the impatient man he used to be.

The delay added to the anticipation.

When they entered the bridal chamber, he didn't pay much attention to the details of the incredibly ornate ostentation of the decor. It was like squinting into bright sunshine. It took him a moment to realize the Doge, or mayhap his duchess, had evidently provided a bevy of maidservants for Zara. He tasted his disappointment. "I wanted to remove your gown," he whispered.

She gave him a woeful look in return, but was whisked away behind a screen by her giggling sister and the excited maids before she had the chance to reply or protest.

Jakov took him by the arm. "I'm afraid the groom will have to make do with me and Bruno."

There was a suspicious glint in his friend's eye, but Kon admitted inwardly Jakov had become like a brother to him, and Bruno was in fact his brother-by-marriage. They were a welcome substitute for his family.

They led him into a small alcove behind another folding screen.

"Get on with it," Jakov urged.

Evidently, he wasn't going to enjoy being undressed by Zara this night. The pleasure would have to wait for another day.

He obediently peeled his tunic over his head and handed it to Jakov. "Satisfied?"

"Shirt, boots and leggings."

He hopped around, removing his boots, took off his shirt, then carefully eased the leggings over his arousal.

Jakov's reaction was predictable. "I see Zara is going to be pleased with her gift."

Titters and sounds of movement from the other side of the screen indicated his bride was being tucked into bed. The women exited the chamber in a flurry of rustling skirts and excited whispers and suddenly all was silent.

His head full of the notion of his bride awaiting him, Kon impatiently looked around the alcove for a bed-robe. Finding none he turned to his friend. Jakov was no longer grinning. Bruno had shoved down his leggings and was pointing to his flaccid manhood. "Small," he said with a shrug.

How to explain what was going on to this innocent young man? Thankfully, Jakov thrust Kon's shirt into his hands and he quickly covered his private parts with the garment.

"Sorry, Bruno," the Croat explained, hurrying to help the frowning lad cover himself. "Only Kon is getting undressed. For Zara."

Kon stood like an idiot with his shirt clutched to his manhood while Bruno stared, but he saw the moment understanding dawned in the young man's eyes. He contorted his face into what might have been a wink, then rushed out from behind the screen, accidentally brushing against it. It toppled over with a loud clatter.

Bruno ran to the bed, kissed his gaping sister who was halfway out of bed, and made for the door. He paused in the open doorway, impatiently beckoning Jakov.

The Croat executed a bow worthy of a count. "That, I believe, is my signal to depart."

Chuckling loudly, the mischief makers exited arm in arm, leaving Kon standing naked with the shirt still clutched to his body. Zara stood beside the bed, raking her eyes over him.

He drank in the vision. Long, black tresses flowed over bare shoulders; the flickering flame of the candle on the night stand illuminated every curve of her nakedness beneath the flimsy nightgown; the startled expression of her blush revealed uncertainty, surprise, longing.

The impatient, hungry Kon rose up in his breast. He tossed the shirt over his shoulder, spread his arms wide and proudly displayed his body.

A BEDDING

Zara recognized the hunger in Kon's eyes, but wasn't afraid. The naked male beast stalking her was magnificent, a bronzed god who had vanquished the powers of hell that had tried to destroy him.

He hadn't come through his ordeal unscathed. His beautiful body would long bear the scars inflicted on him by the slaver; but his once-troubled soul was at peace. She would never meet a man who cared more deeply for the feelings of others. Her body and her soul were safe in his hands and she was more than ready to surrender to him.

The notion sent desire spiralling up her thighs and into her womb as they stood facing each other, noses almost touching. He pulled loose the ribboned shoulder ties holding her nightgown in place, but never took his eyes off her face as the silk slipped silently to the carpet.

After many years of trying to disguise her female attributes, she now had an urge to strut around the chamber, hips swaying, back arched.

She stepped out of the garment, intending to put her arms around his neck and melt into him. "Make me a woman," she whispered.

He put his warm hands on her arms and held her away. "You are already a woman. Tonight you'll become my woman, but let me look at you first."

Breathing steadily, he let his eyes wander over her breasts, down her belly to her mons as if he was studying an exquisite work of art.

Her racing heart nigh on stopped beating when he growled and fell to his knees, pushing her back gently onto the bed. His arms were suddenly gripping her thighs, his mouth on her most intimate place, lapping, sucking, driving her wild with need of him. She pressed her fingertips into his shoulders, her rapture heightened by his gentle strength. She moaned when his tongue found the place connected to every fibre of her being. "Yes, yes," she growled in a husky voice she didn't recognize as he licked and licked and licked.

The intensity of the indescribable feelings was too overwhelming. She needed him to stop, but her heart would shatter if he did.

Her nipples pouted to be touched, her toes twitched, the soles of her feet warmed. She was climbing, climbing, climbing, barely able to breathe. She reached the top of the mountain, held safe in his arms when she fell into a golden abyss of bliss.

Her mouth was too dry to tell him she needed him inside her, but he understood. His manhood carried her to mindless ecstasy. He thrust slowly at first, then faster and more deeply as she urged him on, matching the pace he set.

She'd been forewarned to expect pain, but there was none, only the supreme joy of at last being one with the man she'd craved since the first moment she set eyes on him.

She'd always considered men were brutish, unrefined creatures. She relished every bead of sweat on Kon's back, every grunt, every flex of his muscles, every pulse of his manhood deep inside as he pumped his essence into her happy womb.

Self-control had long been her watchword, her mantra. Now she babbled her euphoria, uttering words she didn't know she knew. He shouted something in German before collapsing on top of her, gasping for breath. She hugged him tightly for long minutes, her sheath still pulsing even after he slowly slipped from her body.

"You'll have to teach me your language," she murmured, twirling a finger in his hair.

When he raised up on his elbows she was

humbled by the love in his eyes as he gazed into hers. "*Gott sei dank*," he replied with a sleepy smile, "it means *Thanks be to God.*"

~ ~ ~

Recalling Zara's taste, her breast in his hand, her aroma—these memories had kept Kon's spirit alive in the darkest of days.

Dreams of lying abed with her had filled his nights ever since their meeting.

None of his reveries came close to the ecstasy of being one with the woman he adored.

He gazed into her eyes, humbled by the love shining in the emerald depths.

The candles eventually guttered out as they cuddled together. He listened to her breathing, played with her hair, nibbled her ear.

"I can hear your heart beating," she whispered.

"It beats for you," he replied, his male urges already stirring again.

As if sensing his need, she pressed her breasts against his chest and gently cupped his sac. "I want you," she said softly.

Kon had never allowed himself to dream he might one day marry a woman of passion, a wife who would bring him the fulfilling intimacy his liberal-minded parents boasted of sharing. In the army he'd known many men who complained of their wives' reluctance in the bedchamber.

Zara was in his blood, but it elated him that he was also in hers. He lifted one breast to his lips and suckled, hard.

She moaned in response. It was the beginning of a long and beautiful night of sexual gratification.

~ ~ ~

Four servants bearing trays of food tiptoed discreetly into the chamber. Zara had lain awake since dawn, listening to Kon snore softly, his warm breath tickling her back.

She sat up and pulled the linens to her neck while the smiling maids set out the food on the elegant table in one corner. Could they tell she'd been transformed overnight from a virgin who knew nothing of congress with a man to a wanton who needed her husband's manhood inside her again and again and again?

Kon stirred and stretched. She covered his naked chest lest she be tempted to kiss his nipples and sift her fingers through the soft hair while servants looked on.

"Good morning, *Signora* von Wolfenberg," one of the maids crooned. "If you and your *husband...*"

She glared at the other three when they giggled.

"...If you would like to break your fast, we will refresh the linens."

Yawning, his hair tussled, Kon propped himself up on his elbows. "I suppose some wedding rituals are the same in every land," he said with a wry smile.

She wasn't sure what he meant, but her immediate concern was their nudity. Her nightgown lay wherever it had fallen and Kon couldn't very well get out of bed with a shirt clutched to his private parts.

She hadn't noticed a fifth maid standing by the door, arms laden with bed-robes. The girl bustled forward at a signal from the senior maid and shyly handed a bed-robe first to her and then one to Kon.

He helped her slip her arms into the garment, hopped out of bed, apparently not as concerned with his nakedness in front of the maids as she had been, and shrugged on his bed-robe.

He came around the bed, kissed her sweetly and offered his hand.

"What did you mean by wedding rituals?" she said softly as she got out of bed.

He winked and lifted the linens to reveal the proof of her lost virginity. "In Saxony, this sheet would be up the flagpole by now."

Mortified, she covered the telling stain. "We can't let them see it."

He squeezed her hand. "We don't want there to be any doubt you were indeed a virgin bride, do we?"

She leaned against him as desire heated her body. "No," she conceded.

"Besides," he said with a wink, "these young women will be mightily disappointed if we deny them their appointed task."

GETTING TO KNOW YOU

Kon escorted his bride to the table laden with food and moved his chair until they were side by side.

Eyeing the busy servants, she reached for a chunk of bread, but he stayed her hand. "It will be my great pleasure to feed you," he said.

She shook her head. "Not in front of the maids," she whispered.

He feigned a pout. "Zara, you need no longer be afraid to be your true self. You're a beautiful woman. Indulge me."

She capitulated with a nervous smile. "I've played the role of the head of household for too long."

He grinned. "You have me now."

After she'd taken a bite of the bread and ham from his fingers, he wished the maids would finish and leave.

She clenched her hands together. "They're too slow."

Their eyes met and they smiled like two conspirators.

"I suppose we can't lie abed the whole day," he conceded when it seemed the maids were dilly-dallying.

"Why not? That's the point of three days of feasting. The guests enjoy themselves, all the while happily aware the bride and groom are busy getting started on the next generation."

She'd spoken in jest, but he decided it was time to shoo out the servants. As soon as he got to his feet, they gathered up the soiled linens and scurried out.

He unfastened the belt of his robe and threw it on the chair. "I suppose they sensed my impatience."

She stared at his arousal. "I still can't believe your whole length fits inside me."

He looked down at his *rute*, arched a brow and offered his hand. "We evidently need another demonstration."

~ ~ ~

Zara had never in her life stayed in bed for a whole day, but she relished every moment of the days and nights she and Kon spent getting to know each other better.

She lay face down on the bed, drooling as he trailed his fingertips along her spine, over and over. She shivered with anticipation when he changed to massaging her thighs, his thumbs parting her cheeks to open her woman's place to his gaze. She squealed with delight when he raised her hips and impaled her sheath from behind, squeezing her nipples as he thrust and thrust, uttering endearments in his own language she knew in her joyful heart he would never whisper to anyone else.

They bathed with rosewater from the ewer, each lovingly cleansing the other.

He taught her intimate German words, showed her where he loved to be touched and how to bring him to the brink of ecstasy with her hand and her mouth. She savored swirling her tongue along the silky length of his *rute* and suckled the taste of an aroused male like a purring kitten.

Servants brought food and drink from time to time—roasted pheasant, peacocks and quail, quinces cooked with cinnamon, olives. They placed the food on the table, but as soon as they were alone again, Kon carried the victuals to the bed and they sat crosslegged, feasting on the sight of each other's nakedness.

Each time Kon bit into an olive he declared his intention to have the fruit at every meal, since the tree had saved his life.

That led to mention of the blue cave and his eternal gratitude to God his *rute* hadn't been stained permanently blue.

That led to laughter, and inevitably to further

intimacy.

She wanted the sojourn to go on forever, but on the last night as they lay together, contended and sated, he asked, "So, my love, I suppose I will learn on the morrow what the third step is in a Venetian wedding?"

She cuddled closer, inhaling the scent she'd come to recognise as his alone. "The bride removes to the groom's home."

He chuckled, stroking her arm with his fingertips. "That might take a while."

"Since your home is far away, I suppose we'll have to change the tradition. You will move into the Polani apartments."

THE VENETIAN WAY

Early on the morrow, they received an unexpected visit from Zara's uncle and his wife. They sat up quickly and drew the linens to their chins as the Polanis paraded in unannounced with a retinue of servants laden with clothing. Two more followed toting a large wooden bathtub, then four footmen entered carrying buckets of steaming water.

Kon wondered what the reaction would have been had they been interrupted in an intimate position. He should be used to things being done differently in Venezia.

"Ah, young love," her uncle gushed. "A gift from my wife and myself," he explained as the servants laid out the garments across the bottom of the bed. "I trust you are ready for the move. Your guests await you in the hall ready to send you on your way."

Kon was astounded to hear anyone was still awake and on their feet after three continuous days of eating and drinking, but he supposed Venetians were used to such festivities.

Zara bristled beside him, evidently as surprised as he at the visit. "Thank you, *zio*."

The duchess seemed to detect the hint of annoyance in Zara's voice before her husband and took his arm to lead him out. The servants traipsed behind. The footmen poured the water and exited.

Zara leapt out of bed and hurried to the tub. "Much as I loved being sponged with rosewater, a bath is tempting."

He joined her, more interested in the prospect of washing her hair than inspecting a badly needed new wardrobe of tunics. "I'll help you bathe."

~ ~ ~

Dishevelled and looking anxious, Jakov hurried to greet them when they entered the hall.

"Sorry we are tardy," Zara said. "I took a bath, then had to wait for my hair to dry, and…"

"One thing led to another," Kon interrupted with a sly grin.

Jakov waved off the jest like a pesky gnat. "Yes, well, I have been summoned to the council chambers. They've apparently reached a decision in my case." He spread his arms wide. "I'm in no fit state after this lengthy celebration of yours, whereas you look splendid."

Zara linked arms with him. "Don't worry. I

suspect most of the *sapientes* who came to the wedding will be slightly the worse for wear. The important thing is you will have satisfaction before you leave for home."

Kon agreed. "She's right."

Jakov raked a hand through his hair. "I am not hopeful."

She squeezed his arm. "At least you will have an answer."

Exuberant well-wishers flocked around the newly-weds and it was a while before they were eventually allowed to take their leave and make their way to the council chambers.

The doors stood open. "We are expected," Zara murmured.

Smiling jovially, her uncle welcomed them and bade them sit. The *sapientes* in attendance nodded benevolently. "It's a good omen," she confided to Kon as they took their seats at the table.

"Count Jakov of Istria," the head of the council intoned.

Jakov stood.

Zara closed her eyes, a shiver racing up her spine when she recalled the vivid horror of his son's drowning. She prayed he would be granted justice.

"On behalf of our beloved Doge and *La Serenissima*, we offer our apologies for the crime perpetuated against you and your son and your people. Istria is a valued neighbor, and we give assurances that attacks on your person and your property will never happen again."

Jakov bowed slightly in acknowledgement.

Kon bristled. "Surely there is more than that," he hissed. "They must have uncovered who committed the heinous act if they can give such an assurance."

A dreadful premonition caused a pulse to throb in Zara's throat. If the perpetrators were linked to some powerful, untouchable person...

The councillor cleared his throat after a brief glance at the Doge. "In recompense, the *Serene Republic* grants to the Counts of Istria in perpetuity free and open access to her trading routes in the Adriatic and Mediterranean Seas and protection from piracy."

Kon seemed somewhat placated. "Well, it's something, I suppose," he muttered.

Zara fidgeted with the cuffs of her new gown. The generous gesture only confirmed her suspicions.

"Be assured the criminals have been punished."

Some insignificant minion had likely paid with his life.

Jakov stood stock still.

Kon clenched his jaw. "He wants the identity

of the men who ordered the attack."

The Croat would receive no satisfaction.

"We thank you for your forbearance," the councillor concluded, "and wish you godspeed on your journey home."

"Godspeed," the other men parroted before rising as one and filing out behind the Doge.

Jakov slumped into his seat, propped his elbows on the table and rested his forehead in his palms. "It is someone too powerful to touch."

His words echoed her fears, but all that emerged from her dry throat was, "It's the Venetian way."

She acknowledged her husband would pursue justice for future victims of such travesties with the tenacity of a bloodhound. She was immensely proud of his stance against slavery, but many of her fellow countrymen wouldn't take kindly to interference from someone they deemed an outsider.

However, he had been willing to sacrifice everything for her. She resolved to stand by him, no matter the cost.

BRUNO'S FLEET

Kon was preoccupied with what he perceived to be an inadequate resolution to the crime that had cost Jakov his son's life. He scarcely paid attention when Zara excitedly ushered him through the entry to the Polani apartments.

Bruno rushed to greet him. "Kon," his brother-by-marriage shouted, hugging him tightly.

The effusive welcome jolted him back to reality. This was an important occasion for his bride and he'd thoughtlessly deprived her of the pleasure of bringing him home. He returned the hearty embrace. "Brother! Are you going to show me around?"

Bruno stepped back and clapped his hands, but then looked at Zara. "May I?"

"Of course," she replied with a broad smile.

The wealth of the family he had married into struck Kon full force as they toured the hall, the dining room, the kitchens, the solar. Bruno offered no explanation except to say *We eat here*, or *They cook here*, or *For guests*.

It became apparent he was saving his enthusiasm for his own chamber. Eyes bright, he bounced up and down on the bed. "I sleep here."

Next he opened the creaky doors of an enormous armoire to reveal hundreds of tunics. "Mine."

Blushing, he pointed to an alcove hidden by a screen. "Pee there," he whispered behind his hand.

Then he knelt in front of a large iron trunk and pulled Kon down beside him. A questioning glance at Zara's enigmatic smile revealed nothing.

Bruno opened the lid and took out a wooden replica of a small cog. He held it up for Kon's inspection like an offertory at a Mass. "*Ottavia*," he said with great reverence.

Kon thought perhaps the toy belonged to his younger sister, but then he noticed the name painted in tiny gold letters on the side. "I see," he said, accepting the ship.

Bruno retrieved another replica. "*Zara*," he explained, grinning at his sister.

Kon swallowed the lump in his throat as he put aside the first ship and accepted the cog named for his bride. "Beautiful, like her namesake."

Bruno nodded vigorously.

A succession of model ships followed, some large, some small. "He's got the whole fleet," Zara explained softly. "My father had them carved for him."

Finally, Bruno stood and reached into the bottom of the trunk. Kon instantly recognised the replica he extracted.

"*Nunziata*," they all declared at once.

They shared laughter, but as Kon stared at the Polani fleet arrayed before him he understood for the first time the awesome responsibility Zara had carried on her slender shoulders.

His heart filled with pride and a determination to do everything in his power to be the partner she deserved.

~ ~ ~

Zara had a feeling Kon now realized the scope of the responsibility he had accepted, but she wasn't worried. He had inner strengths she would always be able to rely on.

She took his hand and pulled him to his feet. "I claim the right to show my husband his new chamber," she told Bruno.

Engrossed in his collection of ships, her brother made no objection.

They tiptoed out of the chamber. She paused and put her arms around his neck. "Most people have no notion how to treat Bruno," she whispered. "I love you for the kindness you've shown him."

He circled her waist. "I have to admit I was nervous at first, and it's a temptation to speak to him as if he's a child. But he isn't, and he knows he isn't."

She leaned her forehead against his, relief flooding her veins. "Many men would have had him shut away."

He cupped her face in his hands. "You know me better than that."

"I do," she admitted, sniffling back the threatening tears.

He took her hand. "Now, let's see this chamber where I am going to spend my life making love to the most beautiful woman in the whole of Venezia."

She pouted, feigning annoyance.

"Sorry, the most beautiful woman in the entire world."

EPILOGUE

Six months later.

With one foot braced atop a rowing thwart, Kon clamped a hand on Lupomari's shoulder. "Congratulations, she looks wonderful. Like a new ship."

The captain thrust out his chest, but gestured to his steersman. "Couldn't have completed the *Nunziata's* refurbishment without Rospo's skills."

Kon shook Rospo's hand. "Thank you indeed. Zara will be thrilled when I describe what you've achieved. It's time we considered making you captain of your own cog."

The green tinge of the gruff steersman's face changed briefly to some indescribable color, but he said nothing.

Lupomari eyed him curiously. "A fine choice," he said thoughtfully, "though I will sorely miss him. Is *Signora* von Wolfenberg of the same mind?"

It wasn't the first time someone in the employ of the Polani fleet had politely intimated he might not have the ultimate authority, and probably wouldn't be the last, but he rather enjoyed the diplomatic game. He was his father's son. "*Signora* Zara is indisposed, as you know, and understands fully the Venetian docks are no place for a woman with child."

He refrained from mentioning the tantrum that had erupted when he'd forbidden her presence at the inspection of the refurbished *Nunziata*. Living with a woman used to having her own way was sometimes a diplomatic tour-de-force in itself.

He looked up to the forecastle. Bruno stood there with legs braced and hands clasped behind his back, looking out to sea. He made a silent promise—one day he would take his brother-by-marriage on a voyage. Sailing was in his blood.

He pointed to the forecastle. "I've discussed the matter with the master of the fleet and he is in full agreement."

Rospo followed his gaze. A rare smile broke out on his face. At least Kon thought it might be a smile. "*Sì*," he croaked.

"Very well," Lupomari replied with a hint of impatience. "I await your instructions. In the meantime, we must catch the noon tide if we are to make it to Istria before nightfall."

Kon scanned the cargo. The *Nunziata* was

crammed with every resource Jakov's missives had indicated his people lacked. "You're right. It's a short voyage, and you've fair weather." He beckoned Bruno, and together they left the ship, though the young man's sullen pout and dragging feet betrayed reluctance.

He put an arm around his brother's shoulders as they walked along the dock. "Zara is waiting anxiously. You can describe the refurbishments to her. We'll practice skimming stones on the way."

This seemed to lift Bruno's spirits but the frown returned when they were stopped by a man he didn't recognize, a wealthy merchant by the look of his garb.

"*Mein Herr* von Wolfenberg?"

Being addressed in his own language took him completely by surprise. "*Ja*," he replied hesitantly.

The man bowed, then produced a slim metal tube from his sleeve. "Ruprecht Klauber, from Hamburg. I have a letter for you. From your family."

~ ~ ~

Zara rolled her eyes and wiped her brow. "You're not listening," she complained after the third unsuccessful attempt to extricate her body from the armchair in her chamber.

Ottavia dragged her attention away from the

document on her lap. "I'm sorry. I was reading Jakov's letter. What did you say?"

Zara prayed for patience and pasted a smile on her face. "I requested your help getting out of this chair. You've read the missive at least ten times."

Ottavia chuckled indulgently. "He misses me."

Zara couldn't fathom how a sophisticated, mature nobleman like Jakov might be interested in her selfish sister, but she had other things to occupy her thoughts, like how she was going to endure another three months of pregnancy.

Ottavia came to her feet and offered a hand. "You're already huge," she said, as if she'd read Zara's thoughts. "Do you think it might be twins?"

Feeling slightly dizzy once she was on her feet, Zara clung to her sister. She had considered the possibility. "Kon told me his mother was a twin."

As if conjured by the mention of his name, her husband entered the chamber. But his pallor was alarming. Her knees buckled and she slumped back into the chair. "What's wrong? Is it the *Nunziata*?"

He stared hard at Ottavia. "Can you leave us alone, sister?"

She frowned but took her leave immediately.

Zara clenched her fists. "I can't bear this. What is it?"

He held out a trembling hand. A small metal tube lay in his palm. "It's a letter. From Wolfenberg."

"At long last," she exclaimed. "What does it say?"

He shook his head. "I haven't had the courage to open it."

She understood. He loved his family dearly and feared he had disappointed them. "Shall I read it to you?"

Relief shone in his eyes as he handed her the tube. She squealed when he scooped her up as if she were a feather and sat in the chair with her in his lap, one big hand on his babe. "No matter the contents of this missive," she assured him, pulling the parchment from its sheath, "remember I love you, and nothing will ever change that."

He inhaled deeply. "Could it be twins?"

She smiled and unrolled the document.

Konrad, my dearest brother.

"Must be from Sophia," he said. "Johann and Lute wouldn't address me as dearest."

We are more than relieved to hear you are safe and well. Your Zara sounds like the perfect partner for you, and who could have imagined my pious little brother would marry the mistress of a fleet? We are glad you are happy.

"Huh," he murmured.

She scanned the next few lines and swallowed the lump in her throat before continuing.

Brandt and I travelled to Wolfenberg when Johann informed us Papa was dying. He passed away a fortnight since. Do not be sad. You are aware it was his dearest wish to be reunited with Mama in the hereafter.

Zara had never known Kon's parents, never met his siblings, but her hands trembled and tears blurred her vision as her husband shook with the effort of controlling his emotions.

Please be comforted, Konrad Dieter. Papa died with your letter in his hands and a smile on his face. I believe sheer determination kept him alive until he was assured you were safe. Your name was the last thing he uttered.

Konrad stiffened and became so still she feared he had stopped breathing. Her rapidly beating heart calmed when his thumb began to stroke her belly. She hurried on.

Johann is Count von Wolfenberg now, of course. He and Kristina are well, as are Lute and Francesca. Imagine Lute is a count! And a good one according to Johann. We are all doing our part to populate the world with more little Rödermarks and von Wolfenbergs.

You are forever in our hearts and we hope you and

Zara will travel to visit us one day.

God be with you.

Your loving sister, Sophia Agneta, Countess Rödermark.

Zara put her arms around her beloved husband and knew the burden of guilt he'd carried for too long had lifted from his shoulders. "Yes, I believe you've fathered twins," she whispered.

"*Gut*," he replied.

He carried her to the bed and they clung together until the shadows lengthened.

HISTORICAL NOTES

MEDIEVAL RELIGION

As you've read, the question of faith dominates Kon's life. It's not the intention of the story to promote one religion over another, or indeed to promote religion at all. The Church played a major role in every facet of medieval life and my goal was to probe into the mind of a medieval man who has lost his previously unquestioned faith in his God and in himself.

IMBECILE

Political correctness precludes the use of this word nowadays, but even in the early twentieth century it was used by census takers in England to describe children in a household who were mentally challenged. My great grandparents had a son who was severely injured in an accident that resulted in brain damage. On the 1891 census he is described as "Delicate", but on the 1901 census he is referred to as an "Imbecile."

COG

The workhorse of early medieval shipping.
https://en.wikipedia.org/wiki/Cog_(ship).
With their flat-bottomed hulls, cogs were ideal
for navigating among shallow, tidal areas. Cogs
were often brought in at high tide and left high
and dry to be unloaded.

STEORBORD AND LARBORD

Today, Starboard and Port. These terms come
from old boating practices. Before ships had
rudders, they were steered by use of a
specialized oar. This oar was held by a sailor
located towards the back of the ship. However,
like most of the rest of society, there were many
more right-handed sailors than left-handed
ones. This meant that the right-handed sailors
holding the steering oar used to stand on the
right side of the ship. The word starboard
comes from Old English steorbord, literally
meaning the side on which the ship is steered.
The old English term steorbord descends from
the Old Norse words stýri meaning "rudder"
and borð meaning "side of a ship". Similarly,
the term for the left side of the boat, port, is
derived from the practice of sailors mooring on
the left side (i.e., the larboard or loading side)
so as to prevent the steering boards from being
crushed. Because the words larboard and

starboard sounded too similar to be easily distinguished, larboard was changed to port.

MAKURIA (NUBIA)

There is good information on the Internet about the African kingdoms of the Nile south of Egypt. Egypt and Makuria developed close and peaceful relations when Egypt was ruled by the Fatimids. The Shi'ite Fatimids had few allies in the Muslim world, and they turned to the southern Christians of Nubia as allies. Fatimid power also depended upon the slaves provided by Makuria, who were used to man the Fatimid army. Trade between the two states flourished until circa 1171AD.

RAGUSA

Ragusa was the medieval name of the walled city of Dubrovnik.

FELOZ

This was the name of an actual slave ship from another, perhaps even darker time in history. Take a deep breath before you read http://www.eyewitnesstohistory.com/slaveship.htm.

KERKYRA

Better known as the island of Corfu.

EARTHQUAKES

The Ionian Islands are situated on one of Europe's most notorious faults, capable of producing earthquakes causing widespread damage and considerable loss of life.

The island of Zakynthos (Zante) suffered a series of four severe earthquakes in August 1953, resulting in the total destruction of its infrastructure. The third and most destructive of these quakes, registering 7.3 on the Richter Scale, had its epicentre directly on the southern tip of the nearby island of Kefalonia, also causing widespread destruction there.

Starting in the early morning hours of 4 April 2006, a series of moderate to strong earthquakes occurring on an almost daily basis began shaking the entire island. On 11 April, however, the phenomenon intensified in both magnitude and rate of events. At 03:02 local time of that day, a powerful, magnitude 5.7 earthquake hit the area, only to be followed by an even stronger tremor, registering 5.9 on the Richter Scale, at 8:30 p.m.

That same evening, two more earthquakes shook the region, sending scores of terrified people into the streets. The earthquakes had a preliminary moment magnitude of 5.8 and 5.4 respectively.

BLUE CAVE
Numerous natural "Blue Caves" are cut into cliffs around Cape Skinari on the northern tip of Zante. They are accessible only by small boat and weren't actually discovered until 1897. I changed the location of Kon's blue cave to the south-western tip of the island in order to bring it closer to the tarpits of Keriou. There are caves in this location but they are not the famous Blue Caves.

TAR
Naturally occurring in this case and more likely what we know today as bitumen or asphalt from the Greek ἄσφαλτος *ásphaltos*.

NARENTINES
https://en.wikipedia.org/wiki/Narentines will lead to good information on these medieval pirates.

DOGE OF VENICE
https://en.wikipedia.org/wiki/Doge

BASILICA DI SAN MARCO
This popular tourist attraction was originally built as the Doge's private chapel, though of course the building that stands today is larger and more elaborate.

ISTRIA
https://en.wikipedia.org/wiki/Istria

ROSPO
You guessed it—Italian for "toad".

ABOUT ANNA

Thank you for reading *Faithful Heart*. If you'd like to leave a review where you purchased the book, and/or on Goodreads, I would appreciate it. Reviews contribute greatly to an author's success.

I'd love you to visit my newly revamped website and my Facebook page, Anna Markland Novels. Tweet me @annamarkland, join me on Pinterest, or sign up for my newsletter.

Passion conquers whatever obstacles a hostile medieval world can throw in its path. My page-turning adventures have earned me a place on Amazon's All-Star list.

Besides writing, I have two addictions-crosswords and genealogy, probably the reason I love research. I am a fool for cats. My husband is an entrepreneur who is fond of boasting he's never had a job. I live on Canada's scenic west coast now, but I was born and raised in the UK and I love breathing life into European history.

Escape with me to where romance began.

I hope you come to know and love my cast of

characters as much as I do.

I'd like to acknowledge the assistance of my critique partners, Reggi Allder, Jacquie Biggar, Sylvie Grayson and LizAnn Carson.

MORE ANNA MARKLAND

If you prefer to read sagas in chronological order, here's a handy list for the Montbryce family books.

Conquering Passion—Ram and Mabelle, Rhodri and Rhonwen

If Love Dares Enough—Hugh and Devona, Antoine and Sybilla

Defiant Passion-Rhodri and Rhonwen

A Man of Value—Caedmon and Agneta

Dark Irish Knight—Ronan and Rhoni

Haunted Knights—Adam and Rosamunda, Denis and Paulina

Passion in the Blood—Robert and Dorianne, Baudoin and Carys

Dark and Bright—Rhys and Annalise

The Winds of the Heavens—Rhun and Glain, Rhydderch and Isolda

Dance of Love—Izzy and Farah

Carried Away—Blythe and Dieter

Sweet Taste of Love—Aidan and Nolana

Wild Viking Princess—Ragna and Reider

Hearts and Crowns—Gallien and Peridotte
Fatal Truths—Alex and Elayne
Sinful Passions—Bronson and Grace; Rodrick and Swan

Series featuring the stories of the Viking ancestors of my Norman families
The Rover Bold—Bryk and Cathryn
The Rover Defiant—Torstein and Sonja
The Rover Betrayed—Magnus and Judith

Novellas
Maknab's Revenge—Ingram and Ruby
Passion's Fire—Matthew and Brigandine (2016) in Hearts Aflame
Banished—Sigmar and Audra (2016)

Caledonia Chronicles (Scotland-The Stewart Kings)
Book I Pride of the Clan—Rheade and Margaret
Book II Highland Tides—Braden and Charlotte
Book 2.5 Highland Dawn—Keith and Aurora (a Kindle Worlds book)
Book III Roses Among the Heather—Blair &Susanna, Craig & Timothea

The Von Wolfenberg Dynasty (medieval Europe)
Book 1 Loyal Heart—Sophia and Brandt
Book 2 Courageous Heart—Lute and Francesca
Book 3 Faithful Heart—Kon and Zara

If you like stories with medieval breeds of dogs, you'll enjoy If Love Dares Enough, Carried Away, Fatal Truths, and Wild Viking Princess. If you have a soft spot for cats, read Passion in the Blood and Haunted Knights.

Looking for historical fiction centered on a certain region?
English History—all books
Norman French History—all books
Crusades—A Man of Value
Welsh History—Conquering Passion, Defiant Passion, Dark and Bright, The Winds of the Heavens
Scottish History—Conquering Passion, A Man of Value, Sweet Taste of Love, Caledonia Chronicles
European History (Holy Roman Empire)—Carried Away, Loyal Heart
Danish History—Wild Viking Princess
Spanish History—Dance of Love
Ireland—Dark Irish Knight

If you like to read about historical characters:
William the Conqueror—Conquering Passion, If Love Dares Enough, Defiant Passion
William Rufus—A Man of Value
Robert Curthose, Duke of Normandy—Passion in the Blood

Henry I of England—Passion in the Blood, Sweet Taste of Love, Haunted Knights, Hearts and Crowns

Holy Roman Emperors—Carried Away, Loyal Heart

Vikings—Wild Viking Princess, The Rover Bold, The Rover Defiant, The Rover Betrayed

Kings of Aragon (Spain)—Dance of Love

The Anarchy (England) (Stephen vs. Maud)—Hearts and Crowns, Fatal Truths, Sinful Passions

Scotland's Stewart Kings—Caledonia Chronicles

Jacobites & Mary, Queen of Scots—Highland Tides

Link to Amazon page

CPSIA information can be obtained
at www.ICGtesting.com
Printed in the USA
LVOW08s2141031116
511542LV00015B/520/P